NIOMIE ROLAND

Love Interrupted

This book was professionally typeset on Reedsy.
Find out more at reedsy.com

Contents

Prologue

"You expect me to believe that nothing is going on between you and Lena?" Kaiya asked as she pinched her lips together tightly.

Tyler raked his fingers through his jet-black hair as his smoky gray eyes took in the serene environment that the Roxboro Park offered. A grimace marked his features.

It was 10 pm, way past his curfew on a school night. He was going to be in a lot of trouble for being out so late. Mrs. Page was going to be mad at him. He had received his last warning a few days ago for returning to the shelter past bedtime.

He had promised Miss Page that he would never be late again, and now, he was breaking that promise. However, it couldn't be helped. He needed to straighten things out with Kaiya tonight.

His gaze flickered again to his sixteen-year-old girlfriend, Kaiya, who had her arms crossed at her chest and was sending daggers at him with her lovely dark brown eyes. Her gorgeous figure was clad in black leggings and a gray sweatshirt. Her glorious black hair was pulled back from her beautiful face in a ponytail.

It was amazing that hours before, they had strolled hand in hand through the park. They had walked through the breathtaking landscape, gazing at the beautiful trees and flowers with the other visitors at the park. Kaiya had talked about how marvelous the place was as they settled themselves on one of the park benches. And then he had received a text message, and all hell broke loose.

He lifted his hand to touch her and dropped it. He needed to make her understand that she meant the world to him. They'd had this argument before, and it was beginning to get frustrating.

"Babe, Lena is just a friend. You've got to believe me." A note of desperation laced his voice.

Kaiya eyed him with disbelief in her eyes. Tyler groaned inwardly as his fingers went through his hair again. He drew closer to the stiff frame on the park bench.

"Why are you finding it difficult to accept that I'm telling you the truth?" He clenched his jaw.

Kaiya dropped her hands. "Well, because she has been all over you like a rash. And I haven't seen you doing anything about it." She folded her arms across her chest again and dealt him a look filled with suspicion. "As a matter of fact, I think you've been enjoying all the attention, and only God knows what else you've been enjoying from her."

Her accusation was so off; Tyler couldn't help the stunned laugh that passed from his throat.

"Like seriously? You think Lena and I..." He left the statement hanging.

Kaiya looked away from him. If her skin wasn't smooth caramel, he would have said she was blushing at that moment. Covering the distance between them on the bench, seventeen-year-old Tyler sought to reassure his doubting girlfriend.

He put his arm around her stiff shoulders. She made to move away, but his arms tightened. Defiantly, she focused her gaze away from him, staring at the peaceful lake before them.

Softly, he said, "Babe, please look at me."

He could read the reluctance in her eyes when she eventually settled in on him.

"Babe, I swear to you with everything I hold dear that Lena and I are just friends, nothing more."

"Then why is she always around you, always calling and texting you?"

Tyler let out a deep sigh. Explaining things to Kaiya would be invading Lena's privacy, but since he so desperately wanted her to believe him, he had to.

Kaiya raised her delicately carved brows at him when he remained silent for some moments.

"Lena is having a difficult time at the group home. Things are pretty messy for her right now."

Drawing out of his hold, she fixed him with a pointed stare. "What has that got to do with you? Are you the only one in the group home that she can talk to? There are caregivers there for her to go to with her problems."

Although what Kaiya said was a tad selfish and insensitive, he couldn't blame her. Lena had been super clingy as of late because of her nightmares. Nevertheless, Kaiya didn't understand what it meant to be in a group home. Her parents were wealthy. Her dad owned a multimillion-dollar real estate development company right there in Montreal. Though her parents weren't model ones, Kaiya had a family and stability, unlike him or Lena.

"Kaiya, Lena is just my housemate. I'm like the only person she has to talk to over there."

"Some talk!"

A grin turned the corners of Tyler's lips. "You have no idea how extremely beautiful you look when you're angry."

She poked a finger at his chest. "Don't change the topic, Mister!"

Tyler gathered her reluctant form into his arms again. "There's nothing to talk about anymore, babe. For the last time, Lena and I are just friends."

"Maybe she wants to be more than friends."

Tyler shook his head. His expression became grave. "Well, I don't want to be more than friends with her, and besides, having a romantic relationship with me is the least of Lena's troubles right now, believe me."

Kaiya sighed. Her gaze sought his imploringly. "Are you sure? Cause I kinda got the 'I want Tyler' vibe from her."

Her boyfriend chuckled. "Trust me, babe. I'm a hundred percent sure."

Kaiya lowered her eyes.

"Kaiya," Tyler began softly, "you mean the world to me. I would rather die than cheat on you. I love you too much to do that to you and us."

Tyler wished he had more exceptional words to relay his feelings to his girlfriend. He loved her so much that he had already started daydreaming about a future with her. Even though they were from different economic backgrounds, he was confident that someday in the future, she would become his wife.

"I love you, my princess. You're the only girl for me."

Kaiya raised teary eyes at him. "I love you so much, Tyler. I can't begin to imagine life without you."

"You don't have to because I'll always be here for you," he solemnly declared, dropping his hands from her waist and cupping her face.

"Promise?" She worried her bottom lip.

"I promise," he declared before lowering his head to take her lips.

Her head inclined upward to receive his kiss. At first, the kiss started slowly, as if they were just trying to discover each other. Minutes later, it heightened as Tyler deepened the kiss. His tongue coaxed her lips open and began an exploration of her mouth. His hands moved all over her body, drawing her closer until there was no space between them.

His tongue dipped sensually into her mouth. A loud moan escaped from her lips, sending him into a frenzy of fevered desire. The intensity of the kiss increased as his manhood became rock hard.

Kaiya ran her fingers through his hair, her nails massaging his scalp, and then her fingers caressed his neck down to his shoulders.

A guttural moan left his lips as she caressed him with inexperienced yet sensual hands. He dragged her to straddle his laps. Her eyes widened when her hand made contact with his erection.

A wry smile formed at his lips. What could he say? He wanted her like he had never wanted anything in his life. His passion for her was so wild; he was afraid that he would scare her.

His honorable intentions were swept with the wind when Kaiya, still kissing him like his mouth contained oxygen, reached down and began unbuttoning his shirt. He understood her need to feel his skin; he also yearned to be skin to skin with her. Placing his hands on the hem of her sweatshirt, he lifted it over her head. It tangled in her ponytail, and she paused in trying to remove his shirt to untwist it from her hair.

He helped her take off his shirt and flung it across his shoulders. She giggled.

The sound of it somewhat doused his ardor. His eyes roamed around the park. Although they were in a secluded and dark place, anyone could walk in on them making out.

His mouth opened to tell her that they couldn't continue even though he desperately wanted to. Kaiya forestalled him by placing her hand against the thick bulge in his trousers.

She bucked against him, grinding her hot core across his rigid length, almost making him come undone. When her fingers began working at his belt, he knew he had to stop her, however, regretfully.

"What are we doing, Kaiya?" he whispered with huskiness.

Capturing his lips in an erotic kiss, she answered in a tight whisper. "I don't know, but I don't want to stop."

"Me neither," he answered truthfully.

With a gruff groan, he lifted her and picked up his discarded shirt. Her legs went around his waist as he carried her a short distance behind a huge tree. Spreading his shirt on the grass, he laid her gently on it. As soon as her back touched the ground, her hands grasped his shoulders to draw him to her.

Their lips meshed again as their hands roved all over each other's bodies. Tyler's hands went behind Kaiya's back to unclasp her bra. He freed her breasts and worshipped the pert molds with his eyes for some seconds before lowering his head to catch a nipple.

Kaiya's back arched as his teeth grated softly on her tits before sucking them. She lay abandoned on the grass as he brought her pleasure untold. Then her hands began fumbling with his belt even as his own hands slowly trailed down her body to caress her moist center.

Her sharp intake of breath when he slid his finger into her was intoxicating. Her body rubbed against him as she still struggled to free the thick bulge from his pants. She abandoned her efforts when his fingers began to stroke her swollen flesh. Her legs rose to curl around his waist as his fingers continued to bring her pleasure.

Her moans grew louder, causing him to increase his strokes against her hot, tight sheath. He caught her scream of release just in time with his mouth, preventing their position behind the tree from being discovered by anyone passing by or sitting nearby.

Quickly, his hands worked on his belt and zip, pulling down his boxers along with his pants. He took a moment to place kisses along her exposed shoulders, her throat, her breasts, her flat, taut stomach, the silky black hair covering her core before reaching for the swollen bud.

"Please," Kaiya begged in a strangled voice and then whimpered while his tongue stroked her.

Stopping what he would have loved to do so that she would have a beautiful first experience, he rose with his elbows to the ground and positioned himself between her thighs.

"Babe, this is going to hurt at first," he whispered against her lips.

She nodded with frightened eyes. He decided to go as slowly as he could, his eyes trained on her, watching for any sign of discomfort from her. Even though it might kill him if she wanted him to stop, he would do so instantly.

When her hand went down to grasp his member, it was all the encouragement that he needed. His fingers resumed tracing her wet slit. Then he replaced his fingers with his manhood, slowly pressing against it. Anticipating a scream from her, his lips seized hers as he plunged into her body.

Her body jerked under his, causing him to lie still for some minutes, giving her time to get used to the foreign invasion. His eyes earnestly watched her face from the light the moon provided, skimming the leaves in the trees.

"Babe, are you alright?" he questioned softly, worried about her tightly-shut eyes.

For an answer, she tightened her legs around him, holding him tautly between her thighs. Her hands trailed his muscular back. Taking that as a sign of encouragement even though her eyes were still closed, he withdrew his manhood and entered her again, slowly, trying to rein in the intense emotion that wanted him to go harder and faster.

A muscle jerked in his neck as he slid out again and slid back in, drawing out her passion along with his.

This is pure heaven!

Unbridled pleasure coursed through his body. With each stroke, his desire for her increased. Wave after wave of sensation racked his body. His eyes

6

never left her face. At some point in time, she opened her eyes. The powerful love he saw in their depths was almost his undoing. He almost lost control as his pace increased inside her hot, tight, moist flesh, driving her body forward with the force of his movement.

Suddenly, her body clenched and rippled in wet spasms. The clasping of her flesh around his finally broke his control, and he slammed into her with frenzied movements.

He bent his head and caught her scream as her body convulsed underneath his. Her nails dug deeply into his back as he continued pounding in and out of her.

"Kaiya!" he called in a ragged voice as he found his own release. His body shook uncontrollably as he poured his seed into her, basking in the best feeling in the world.

Back in control again, he pulled his semi-limp manhood out of her and collapsed beside her, drawing her into his arms.

They stayed like that in companionable silence for some minutes. Then rising a little, he cupped her cheek in his hand and said with much tenderness,

"I love you, Kaiya, for all eternity."

"I love you, too, Tyler," she responded with a smile to rival the sun.

Tyler removed the necklace his grandma left him before she died from around his neck, and lifted his girlfriend's head to place it around her neck.

He solemnly affirmed, "This necklace is my promise to you that we'll always be together and I'll always be with you. You will always have my heart, babe."

Tears welled up in her eyes as she elevated the necklace to look at it. His finger caught the lone tear that ran halfway down her cheek.

"I'll treasure it always. Thank you, Tyler. You mean the world to me."

His head descended to capture her lips.

* * *

Two weeks later...

Kaiya sighed as she rubbed fresh red lipstick on her lips, eyeing herself critically on the bathroom mirror. "I can't reach Tyler. I've been trying to get a hold of him all day. He hasn't responded to any of my calls."

"Uh, a slightly bigger problem here," her best friend, Jalissa, grumbled.

Whirling in her friend's direction, Kaiya offered her nervous friend a smile filled with encouragement.

Her phone beeped on the sink at that instant, and she quickly grabbed it. A sigh of disappointment left her lips when she discovered it was just a Facebook message from Kalilah, her sister, who now lived in the States. Not bothering to reply to it, she placed the phone back on the counter and stared at her reflection on the mirror.

Two weeks ago, her relationship with Tyler changed after she gave him her virginity. Never in her wildest dreams had she thought that she and Tyler would get intimate so soon after being together, but she had no regrets. They had been dating steadily for two months, and they'd had sex every day for the past two weeks. They went to motels almost every day in the past two weeks. Last night though, they'd fallen asleep till 2 am. Tyler had freaked out about the time and left. The group home he lived in had strict rules. She hoped he hadn't gotten into too much trouble this time.

Her fingers stroked the beautiful necklace that Tyler gave her that night. She never took it off, not even when she wanted to shower. She had this crazed thinking that she might misplace it if she did and invariably lose Tyler's heart.

Her love for him had grown in leaps and bounds even though her parents didn't care much for him. Her dad had called him a degenerate after finding out he lived in a group home because his mom was an alcoholic. She loved Tyler, though; she was almost bursting at the seams with it, and that was all that mattered.

"OMG, it's positive!"

Her friend's outburst cut into her musings. She turned to look at her wide-eyed friend who was positioned on the toilet seat, holding a pregnancy test strip firmly.

Kaiya shook her head. Her friend had been freaking out all morning, repeatedly saying she believed she was pregnant because her period was a few days late. Distraught, Jalissa had brought home some, maybe ten, pregnancy test kits to allay or confirm her fears.

Being the supportive friend that she was, Kaiya had decided to use one of the tests. Trepidation gripped her when she registered the fear and worry in her friend's eyes.

Pushing herself away from the mirror, she hurried to her friend's side.

"Are you sure?" she questioned softly, gazing at the stick in her friend's quivering hand.

The breath caught in her throat when she saw the two pinks lines. Dear God, Jalissa was pregnant! Oh, no, what was she going to do? Her arm instinctively went around her friend's shoulder.

"Everything's going to be fine, Jalissa. We'll get through this together," she offered, trying to hide the tears in her eyes.

"Kaiya," Jalissa called in a small voice, darting her tongue across her lips, "the test isn't mine. It's yours."

The words exploded in Kaiya's eyes. Her heart stopped beating for a second.

"What?" Her arm fell from her friend's shoulders, and she took a step back fidgeting.

"Mine are those three over there. They're all negative. I was about to throw all of them away when I saw yours," Jalissa explained and quickly rose to her feet.

Kaiya's lips quivered in unison with her hand as she reached for the test strip,

It can't be! It was too soon to tell.

She and Tyler had sex every day for the past two weeks. Granted, they hadn't used protection the first time, carried away in the heat of passion, but they did use protection after that. How possible was it that she would get pregnant just that one time?

Twenty minutes later and two more positive test strips later, Kaiya paced Jalissa's room, clutching the pendant on the necklace Tyler had given her between her fingers.

She was indeed pregnant! She was only sixteen for crying out loud! A baby wasn't a part of her plans. How was she ever going to be a professional ballet dancer if she was saddled with a baby? Her parents would surely kill her. They had blackmailed her older sister into marriage, what would they do to her?

"OMG, my parents will kill me!" Her hand shook as she stared at her phone. "Why the hell isn't Tyler picking up his phone or responding to my text messages?"

Her first instinct had been to call him to inform him that their lives were about to change. But she couldn't get him on the phone, even now!

"What are we going to do?" Jalissa queried from her bed. Her eyes were also red-rimmed like her friend's and her face was wet with tears, too.

Her face ashen with fear, Kaiya shook her head. "I don't know. All I know is that my life is about to change and I doubt very much it's for the better."

Chapter 1

The pain began as a little twinge below her protruding stomach. Gradually, it increased, sending sharp pangs all over her body. She tried opening her eyes, but it appeared as if they were glued shut.

A scream passed from her throat as intense pain racked her body again. Forcing her eyes open, her heart slammed painfully in her chest when she discovered she was in a dark room. She could view nothing except pitch darkness.

Another bout of pain shot through her body. She gasped and tried to rise from the surface she was on to get help. It was all in futility because she couldn't move her body. It seemed like she was chained to the bed.

Hysteria hit her as the bed began to spin.

"Help! Somebody, help me!" she screamed to no avail.

The bed suddenly stopped spinning, and then she found herself in a brightly lit, empty room trying to push out her baby amidst extreme pain. Everywhere was painted in white, and there wasn't an iota of furniture in the place save the bed. Glancing down, she noticed she was in a delivery position. Her knees were upturned; her hands tightly gripped her heels, her face was doused with sweat, yet there was a chill in the large room that sent shivers up to her spine.

"Arrgggghhhh!" she yelled. The urge to push was so overwhelming; she gave in to it.

A thick frown creased her forehead when she pushed and pushed yet her baby didn't come out. Her eyes darted across the room without a door or a window. There was no one to help her. Even if she called for help, who would hear her? The room felt like a mausoleum.

The compulsion to push again as more pain wracked her body consumed her. Pushing with all her might, she fell back on the bed, hoping to feel the baby leaving her body and the pain stopping.

When none of that occurred, she raised her head. Her lips parted in surprise. Striding toward her with a dazzling smile on his face and a bundle in his arms was seventeen-year-old Tyler as boyishly handsome as ever.

"Congratulations, my love," he said to her in a voice that was like ripples in water.

Smiling, she gently carried the blanket from him to gaze lovingly at what it held.

A scream tore out from her throat when she noted that the blanket was filled with nothing but blood.

Kaiya woke up with a start. Beads of perspiration marked her forehead. Her breath came in shortly as her eyes trailed her room. She was no longer in the bright room, and Tyler was nowhere to be found.

Exhaling softly, she pushed herself into a sitting position, grateful that it was only a dream. It had been so vivid; she had feared it was real.

Disbelief crossed her face because she found it hard to believe that her nightmares had returned. Trepidation filled her at the thought that she might start having them almost every night like she experienced after the death of her child. This particular nightmare hadn't plagued her sleep in ages. And there was only one reason for it occurring now.

Tyler Landry!

The return of Tyler to Montreal was the most likely cause of her resurfacing terrible dream! Why in the world did he have to come back? Why now that her life was progressing smoothly?

Kaiya took a moment to reflect on her life after she resolved to pull herself together and forge ahead after the loss of her child. Since she came to terms with her baby's death, her life had been moving forward steadily with several achievements. Everything was going just fine. Her sister had moved back to Montreal as she and her husband reconciled, her dance studio was thriving, her niece and nephew were the absolute cutest toddlers, and her plans to expand her dance school were on track. Granted, she didn't end up as a professional ballet dancer for apparent reasons; however, she was living a fulfilled life nevertheless.

If she was sincere to herself, seeing Tyler again had stirred up memories and nightmares of their past. Though it was said to be a small world, not once had the thought of seeing him again ever crossed her mind. For years, she had pushed the anguish she felt at losing the love of her life and their baby to the recesses of her mind. To think of it was sheer torture, but now she was doing it. All thanks to Tyler showing up at her dance studio two days ago.

She closed her eyes as the image of him standing in her dance studio flashed through her mind.

His features were the same but more advanced. His hair had become darker, his eyes were still a cloudy gray but were now even more penetrating. It appeared that he still worked out to keep fit. His shirt accentuated his broad shoulders and muscular chest. The jeans clung to his legs, heightening the strength of his body. When he had smiled uncertainly at her, she noted the dimple on his right cheek, a feature that used to make her weak in the knees whenever it made its appearance.

Her steps had stumbled to a halt when she returned to the lobby of her dance studio to hand over her fussing niece to her sister. Her breath had drawn sharply against her throat as she set eyes on the man who had broken her heart eight years ago.

"Tyler!" she had called with surprise in her voice.

His deeply penetrating gaze had fallen on her. Cold dark brown eyes had latched onto his own smoky gray ones from across the room. She had stood there and endured the way his eyes trailed her body. Jalissa had come to stand beside her. Kaiya saw it as a show of solidarity, and she was grateful to have her best friend there. Jalissa was the only one in the room that truly had an idea of what she went through when Tyler abandoned her.

"Kaiya," Tyler had said as he confidently strode his six-feet-five-inch frame across the lobby to meet her, ignoring everyone else there. Her name on his lips had brought back painful memories. His voice was more profound than she remembered it.

He had insisted on talking to her privately. Reluctantly and oozing iciness, she had followed him outside after telling him she could only spare him a minute because she had to get back to her dancers.

He said he needed to talk to her about an important matter, and she wondered what it could be.

Maybe he found out, she mused but dismissed her thoughts as impossible since the only people who knew couldn't have told him.

Seeing him again was definitely the cause of the resurgence of her nightmare. She had been enraged yet trapped in his handsome snare the minute she set eyes on him again. Her gaze had been wielded to his lips, remembering the countless times he had brought her neck-deep in passion with them. The familiar scent of him had awakened her senses.

"Yep," she sighed, "he's the cause of my bad dream."

Flinging aside the sheets, she got out of her double-sized bed. Her body, covered in gray slacks and a white and black sweatshirt, bent as she did a few stretches. Then she trudged to the bathroom to brush her teeth.

As the brush moved up and down in her mouth, and as she stared at her reflection in the mirror, she recalled when she and Tyler first met.

It had been at one of the house parties she and Jalissa had snuck out of their houses to attend. The location of the party was close to the group home where Tyler lived.

As the party got heated and boys and girls danced to the rhythm of the latest hit songs, her dance partner had gotten too adventurous and handsy with her. His hands had been all over her body under the pretext of dancing. Incensed when he wouldn't stop, she had wanted to walk away from the dance floor, but he had held her rigidly until a handsome boy had intervened. He had told the tipsy boy to take a hike. The determination and probable menace in the newcomer's eyes had registered in her dance partner's eyes, and he had moved away, cursing and swearing.

Kaiya had thanked her knight in shiny armor before he walked away. A few minutes later, in search of a washroom, she had found the boy who helped her earlier in one of the rooms. The boy, who she got to know later was called Tyler, was in there studying with a book on his laps. Just like her, he had been stunned that the door wasn't locked. Giggling at the look of discomfiture on

14

his face, she had wondered what a teenager like herself was doing studying when a party was going on downstairs.

"Got a big test tomorrow?" she questioned when minutes had elapsed from them gawking at each other.

He had grinned at her, and that was when she experienced the first devastating effect of his dimpled cheek.

"Something like that," he had replied shortly.

Folding her hands across her chest, she had bestowed him with a smile of her own. "A straight-A student, I see."

Chuckling, he shook his head. "Most definitely."

She had found him irresistibly handsome with his jet-black hair, and smoky gray eyes that could eat a girl whole. She thanked him for helping her and teased him some more about studying. They spoke for a bit on trivial things.

Unable to resist, Kaiya then asked him to dance, and he reluctantly agreed. Everything had seemed so magical. They shared their first kiss that night; it had been like a taste of heaven. He had asked her out, and she had all but fallen over him in her rush to answer in the affirmative. Their relationship built up after that.

Kaiya came back from her trip down memory lane to hear her cellphone ringing. Quickly, she finished cleaning up and rushed to her room. She snatched the phone from her bedside table and grimaced a little when she saw who was calling.

It was Marcus – her friend with benefits. Forcing cheerfulness into her voice that she didn't feel, she answered the call. He was calling to see if she would be available for dinner in Torque. Kaiya appreciated his efforts although unwelcomed; she politely declined his offer.

Marcus, she suspected, was beginning to get too attached. She was afraid that he was starting to get the wrong ideas of being in a relationship with her.

They had met at one of her family's charity dinners since he worked for Finn – her brother in law as a real estate agent. She was lonely, he was sexy and saying all the right things. One thing had led to another, and they had ended up in bed. And so, whenever she wanted to scratch the itch, she called him, and they hooked up. Twice now, he had called her up to go on a date.

"No, Marcus, I can't," she said and placed her phone back on the bedside table.

Years ago, she had sworn that she was done with emotional entanglements. Never again would she be caught in such a disastrous web. She made a mental note to break things off with him before his thoughts of them dating went too far.

Once bitten, twice shy.

* * *

Kaiya!

Tyler's mouth curled into a grimace as he remembered the girl who had haunted his dreams for the past eight years. When he made the decision to move back home to Montreal from British Columbia after he got the contract, the first person who had made her presence known in his mind was Kaiya. Not only had she plagued his dreams then, but his thoughts as well. Although every time he thought of Montreal or the place was mentioned, Kaiya always came to mind. But getting the contract which saw to his evident return to the place where he had grown up had only heightened it.

He had envisaged different scenarios of how their first meeting would be after so many years. He had, however, never expected an audience when he walked into her dance school the previous day. He recalled walking into the place and seeing the perplexed faces of Jalissa, Katherine, and another pregnant woman who looked like a younger, darker version of Katherine. Katherine's stare had seemed different, though; it had appeared haunted, but he wouldn't bother trying to decipher what it meant. It was none of his business. He no longer cared what Kaiya's parents thought of him.

Sighing, he strode to the living room's window and stared out into the quiet street. Montreal had changed a great deal from the time he hastily left the place eight years ago. Memories flooded him as he remembered when he departed as a scared and lonely teenager.

After he left Montreal and moved to Vancouver, British Columbia, he started University. Although it was hard to leave his daughter at first, he quickly found a routine with his daughter's mom, Lena. The thought of his late best friend and how she was tragically taken from them always got him wracked with guilt. If only...

He shook his head. It was best to dwell on good memories, not painful ones. Like the wonderful news of his mom who was now ten years sober and his perfect support system.

Thankfully, against all the odds, he had graduated, got mentorship, and through it, he had begun to get contracts from real estate developers. As the demand grew for his architectural expertise, he went into the construction and design end of real estate and eventually became a real estate developer himself. A few smart investments later, and he was now a self-made businessman; investments that made him part of the elite. He had a wonderful daughter; his mom was clearheaded, and he got one of the biggest contracts of his career that would bring him millions. He had a lot to be thankful for despite his poor background. At the moment, he believed he had everything he needed in life. That was the reason he was beginning to reconsider accepting the contract with Finn; Anderson Realty. As a matter of fact, he was beginning to wonder if moving back to Montreal was a good idea.

Tyler turned away from the peaceful view outside and took a sip from his mug of coffee. He knew the reason he was beginning to have second thoughts about his decision. It had something to do with the teenage girl who had grown into a very beautiful woman.

Everything about her seemed perfect. From the dark tresses on her head pulled back in a slick ponytail, to the heart-shaped face, startling brown eyes, pouting lips, and slim physique, she was out-and-out stunning. He had braced himself knowing he would see her eventually, but the effect of just a glance at her was still devastating to his senses nonetheless.

His mouth curled with cold distaste. Beautiful outwardly but a cold heart within. She didn't deserve any reaction from him, and he was pissed that he had gawked at her for minutes on end when she came into the lobby.

He had gone there in the first place to set things straight since he was sure they would be seeing each other because of his daughter. Instead, he had gotten himself seared by her beauty and animosity.

It was by accident that he found out that his daughter had been registered by his mom for ballet lessons in Kaiya's dance school. Finn Tremblay, his new business partner, had mentioned to him the name of Kaiya's dance school, Just Dance, in passing, and then it had clicked that his daughter was registered there.

Gritting his teeth, he had picked up his phone to call his mom to cancel the registration. Then he had paused because his mom would have wanted to know why the change in plans and she would have become suspicious of his motives. She knew only what he had told her about his past with Kaiya, and he wanted it to stay that way in order to avoid being questioned repeatedly by his mom and breaking his darling daughter's heart because she had been very excited to continue her ballet lessons.

Seeing the best recourse was to have a chat with Kaiya to ensure that his daughter was in safe hands, he had decided to go to the dance studio. He didn't want the daughter he loved so much to be treated differently, simply because of their shared history.

The scene flashed through his mind like it just happened a few minutes ago.

"Tyler? What the hell are you doing here?" Jalissa threw at him with savage bite, regarding him as if he was something unpleasant that just crawled out from under a rock.

"Good to see you again, Jalissa, I'm looking for Kaiya." He was determined not to be bothered by the animosity that the woman was exuding in waves.

"Why don't you leave, Tyler? You're not wanted here!"

Tyler sighed inwardly. After so many years, he didn't know whether to be pleased or pissed that Jalissa was still as loyal as ever to her best friend. She was still the watchdog, the bodyguard he had nicknamed the wilding because of her carefree ways.

He was forestalled from replying to the furious woman when he caught a movement from the corner of his eye. Kaiya strode into the room with a girl toddler propped on her hip. The phone she had been talking into fell from her hand. Her jaw dropped, and she froze at the sight of Tyler.

Tyler also became immobilized as he gaped at the woman who used to be his girlfriend when she was much younger. Her beauty seemed to have grown more over the years. She was more beautiful as an adult than she was as a teenager. Even though she still favored leggings and a sweatshirt, her figure had ripened, fleshing out at her hips.

For a long moment, they stared at each other with no words, forgetting that there were others in the room but the two of them. But under the beauty, he could see the underlying sadness in her eyes, and her expression strained. For some reason, he was compelled to fix that sadness, but then he remembered how selfish and heartless she was. His heart hardened.

Snapping out her numbness when the child on her hip called for her mom, she had exclaimed, "Tyler!"

As if her voice broke the invisible hand holding him bound, he called her name too and strolled forward to meet her. She handed the child to the pregnant woman he presumed was her sister, who he had never met before now.

With her eyes shooting icicles at him, she had asked, "What are you doing here?" just as Jalissa came to stand beside her with the same stony glare on her face.

Finn also stepped closer to them to probably protect Kaiya since she was his sister-in-law.

Ignoring the hostility the women were sending his way, he wondered why Kaiya didn't follow her dreams of becoming a ballerina. Before he could stop himself, he said, "You didn't become a professional ballet as you'd always wanted. Why is that?"

His lips ran dry when a pained look crossed her face. The hollowness in her eyes left him regretting why he asked.

Thrusting out her chin and folding her arms across her chest, she remarked, "That's none of your business. Now, for the last time, why are you here?"

Jerking his head back as if she physically hit him, his gray eyes darkened with anger. *How dare she talk to him this way?* He was no longer the poor boy who lived in a group home. Now, they were more than equals. So where did she get off treating him like he was still some social outcast?

Straightening himself to his full height, he nodded at the audience they had and said, "I'd love to speak with you in private. We need to talk about an important matter."

Sizing him up from head to toe as if he were a bug she'd like to squash under her feet, she re-joined with a freezing tone, "Go to hell!"

With that, she left him standing there with a face like a storm cloud and fisted hands. In solidarity, everyone moved out of the place and left him to stew.

Coming back to the present, Tyler wondered why Kaiya was upset with him when she was the one who not only ended their relationship but betrayed him as well.

Snickering, he resolved to make her pay for what she did to him.

Chapter 2

Two days later, Kaiya carefully planned her day as she stepped into her dance studio. She thought of the various dance classes they were scheduled to have. There were bilingual dance programs like mini ballet jazz, ballet jazz, mini hip hop, and hip hop for kids ages 2 to 12 years old, in addition to a prenatal yoga class that Kalilah talked her into developing. She generally stayed away from that section for the sake of her sanity. On weeknights, she led a pole fitness class for different skill levels.

As she strode toward her office, her phone rang. She rummaged through her purse for the device, hoping she would find it before it stopped ringing. Her purse was usually filled with stuff that she didn't need at the end of the day but always felt she had to carry. Consequently, it was typically hard for her to find her phone in it.

Sighing with relief when she at last located it, she saw that it was her mother calling.

"Hey, Mom."

"Hi, Kaiya. How are you?"

"I'm good."

"I just wanted you to know that I'm going on a European cruise. Don't know when I'll be back."

"What? When?"

"I leave in two days."

Kaiya's mouth formed an O, for she was dumbfounded at the suddenness of her mother's trip. It was also quite strange because she had made it known that she wanted to be there for the birth of Kalilah's baby.

"What about Kalilah's baby?" she couldn't help asking as she was still trying to process her mom's news.

"I've already told your sister that I'm leaving. Although she's disappointed, she accepted it. Besides, I might even be back before the baby comes, who knows?" Katherine replied shortly.

Kaiya's forehead scrunched into a frown. It was rather shocking that her mom would just up and leave without giving any reason. Things she knew weren't fine between her parents, so she wondered if that played a role in the woman's sudden decision to take a trip to Europe.

Since she might likely be told it was none of her business, she kept mute. Although she and her mother had drawn closer after the loss of her son, there was still that gap between them that years of neglect had caused.

"Alright, Mom. Have a safe trip."

"Thanks, darling, one more thing. I know I wasn't always the best parent to you girls, but I want you to come out of your head and step out on faith like you use to. Tyler being back could be what you need to heal and move on. Don't shut him out." The call clicked off.

Kaiya stared at her phone, surprised by her mom's sudden trip and surprising advice. Her mom, Katherine, had really been trying since she separated from their father, Richard, but this advice given by her mom would be ignored. She was done with Tyler and had no interest in anything he had to say. Everything good she felt about him had been cremated in her mind, just as their son was.

Shrugging off her dark thoughts, she strode to her office. The small office was done in shades of cream and pale yellow. A small desk and chairs occupied one side of the office while a chaise lounge covered one part of the wall which she laid on whenever she wanted to get her feet up. On one side of the wall were pictures of several ballet dancers, including kids in the school. Another side held her school and registration certificates. There were several paintings on the wall which served to beautify the room.

Kaiya tread the carpeted floor to her table, where she settled down on the swivel chair and stared at the ceiling as she mentally prepared herself for the day.

A knock sounded on the door, and two of her dance teachers came into the room to exchange pleasantries with her. They were going to their respective classes when they saw her come in and wanted to say hi. They left soon after the greetings were over.

They didn't have many students in the mornings because of school and work. The few that came in were handled by other dance teachers.

As the day progressed, Kaiya looked through her accounts. Her dance studio was doing pretty well, and she was happy about it. Years ago, she never thought she would make it this far.

When it was about time for her afternoon dance lessons to begin, she sought out her employees and discussed with them the afternoon lessons. She finished with them, and they dispersed.

As she stood, seeing to different groups of kids, two of her dance teachers joined her when parents dropped off kids for dance lessons.

"Um, Kaiya?" Daisy said quietly.

"Yes, Daisy." Kaiya curved her body a little in her direction.

With a twinge of excitement in her voice, she said, "I'll need to leave before the 6 pm class arrives."

Arching her brows, Kaiya asked, "Why? Is everything alright?"

Grinning, she replied, "It sure is. Perry finally asked me out."

Smiling, her employer remarked, "Good for you, Daisy! You have my permission to leave early to prepare for your date."

"Aww, thanks, Kaiya. You're the best."

Smiling at the twenty-year-old girl, Kaiya turned away. Daisy and her other employee discussed excitedly what the former would wear and other details of the date.

As she listened, Kaiya had a nostalgic feeling of what it used to be like when she was a teenager and asked out on a date. But now, she was contented with just running her dance school for children. She would rather not date anyone now, which reminded her that she needed to end things with Marcus. He had been wanting more from her than she could give, and she didn't want him to think she had led him on by the time he recognized that there was no hope of her changing her mind.

Kaiya exhaled softly as she turned away. She hadn't felt strongly about anyone after Tyler, and she didn't intend on giving her heart to anyone, considering she made a silent promise to her baby to never forget him by loving someone else. And she was determined to keep the promise.

Against her better judgment, her mind drifted to when she found out that she was pregnant in her best friend's bathroom. Now and then, her mind would trail back to that terrifying day.

How scared she had been when she repeatedly saw those two pink lines. When her parents found out by accident and saw how depressed she was, they whisked her away to New Brunswick. She spent the remainder of her pregnancy there in solitude until she gave birth.

It would have been tough, but she had been ready to raise her baby alone. Unfortunately, in the end, there was no baby. When she finally came back to Montreal, she heard from Jalissa that Tyler had left Montreal with Lena to raise their baby. She had felt betrayed by Tyler, who had always insisted that nothing was going on between him and Lena. Little wonder he hadn't bothered replying to any of her messages or returning her calls. He must have discovered that Lena was pregnant at that time and, too ashamed to tell her. He probably believed that ignoring her was the best form of recourse. It hurt to think that he had most likely impregnated her and Lena at almost the same time. The sleazebag had been sleeping with both of girls and denying it.

She wondered for the first time if Lena and Tyler were still together and raising their family. A family she didn't have. Did they have more children? Was their first child a boy or a girl?

Pain wrenched her heart at what might have been if she hadn't lost her baby and if Tyler didn't turn out to be a lying, cheating jerk.

Her mind drifted from her past to the women's group she had recently joined at the insistence of Kalilah. Her sister saw through her efforts in trying to hide that she was fine. The people in the group were people who lost children and they met once a week to discuss their varying feelings and emotions. Kaiya felt she was on the road to permanent recovery, but with the return of her ex-boyfriend, painful memories kept flooding her.

Shaking off the vestiges of her terrible past as she heard children laughing, she went to prepare for the lessons.

* * *

Tyler slid into his jet-black Grand Cherokee jeep and just sat there, staring ahead. Although he was running ragged by the demands of being a single father, he was more than grateful for the opportunity.

He just left the café where he hung out with two of his friends from his group home. He wasn't shocked that they and others that he contacted never made it to college. Coming out of the group home with no family to turn to wasn't ideal. Most of his past group home housemates did odd jobs to make a living. He thanked God for blessing him with his baby girl since she probably saved his life.

Tyler figured that had he remained in Montreal, he wouldn't have been any different from the men he just left at the café.

However, moving back to the place where he grew up and where he had been hurt the most still brought about painful memories. First, he was abandoned by his alcoholic mom, who came back into his life at about the same time his daughter did and then Kaiya. It would be difficult, but he knew he would cope. He just had to, for the sake of his daughter.

Tyler pulled his car into the driveway of his three-family unit in Lexington, Westmount. He couldn't say why of all the houses in Montreal, he had chosen this large family house when it was only just him, Lili and his mom to live in it.

Perhaps it was the homey feeling it provided or perhaps his vanity that he could now afford such a house when he used to live in a group home. It could also just be the architect in him.

The three-storied terraced building boasted of a grand foyer, a sun room, a library with built-in shelves, six bedrooms, an attic, a basement, and a garage. The structure was done in shades of sky blue, white, and light gray. The house was still bare of furniture and finishing because he had been so busy since recently moving back to Montreal he hadn't had time to do that, and he wanted his mother and daughter to come along when shopping. Nevertheless, the building had the convenience of air-conditioning, a sound security system, and high-tech bathrooms. His mother had chosen to live in the basement for her own privacy, even though he had protested.

"Hey Mom," he called as he strode into the kitchen where she was baking cookies.

"Hey, Son," she replied as she removed a batch from the oven.

Tyler climbed on the stool by the counter and reached for one, but his mother tapped his hand with her spatula.

"Ouch!"

"It's hot," she warned, giving him the stern eye look she used to bestow on him when he was much younger.

"I know," he grumbled good-naturedly and reached for it again. It was indeed very hot, so he dropped it on the tray, causing his mother to laugh.

Her laughter, however, sounded strained, so he gave her a queer look. He noted the wrinkles on her forehead and frowned.

"Mom, are you alright?" he questioned with worry lacing his voice.

She raised her brows at him. "Of course, I'm alright? Why wouldn't I be?"

She turned away so hastily it belied her words. Tyler fixed his intense gaze on the slim, petite woman. She pushed back a strand of coffee brown hair from her pixie haircut and kept her honey-brown eyes from his.

Even though it was after the birth of Lili that he and his mother got to be reacquainted, he was attuned to her moods. Something was troubling her. Although she had been sober for over ten years now, he still worried about her.

"Mom, please tell me what's wrong," he urged when she still refused to look at him.

"Nothing," she answered, but he caught a sob in her throat.

He rose from his stool, strolled around the kitchen island to place comforting hands on her shoulders. He gently whirled her around and wasn't surprised to see the tears glazing her eyes.

The worried man dropped his hands. "Mom, please talk to me."

She sniffed and waved a nonchalant hand. "Don't mind me. I'm just being silly."

"Whatever has upset you this much isn't silly to me. Please tell me what's wrong."

Lowering her head, the woman sighed heavily. Then she lifted eyes filled with despair at him.

"I know that you really need the contract and the change is good for Lili, but I must confess that coming back here where my life was a total mess is...is proving very difficult for me."

Tyler nodded. He completely understood what she was talking about. They both had good but terrible memories about Montreal.

"This place reminds me of how my life used to be in the pits. How I was a danger to both you and myself." Raising her hand, she cupped his cheek. "I'm so sorry for the tough childhood you had. If I could do it all again, I wouldn't grieve so hard when your father decided to stay with his wife instead of being with me, which made me take solace in alcohol." Tears rolled down her face. "I will never regret having you because you have been nothing but a blessing to me. I only wish that I sobered up sooner to take care of you instead of allowing you to grow up in group homes. I'm so sorry."

Tyler acknowledged what she meant by wishing she had come back into his life sooner. His mom had suddenly shown up at the apartment he shared with Lena just about when Lili came into their lives. Before then, he and Lena had left the group home and were working at a fast-food joint.

His mom had come there all weepy and apologetic, saying that she had been sober for the past two years and was trying every day to be a better person and mother.

Tyler had been overjoyed to have her in his life just when he needed her most. He had told her the past was forgiven and forgotten and welcomed her back with opened arms.

"We should move to British Columbia for a new start. Montreal doesn't hold pleasant memories."

Tyler had agreed with her, and when he asked his mother if she would like to come along, she had been overjoyed to be invited along and given a second chance. It had been very challenging starting all over again, but with support from both Lena and his mother, he had been able to pull through against all odds.

Sadness flowed within him when he remembered Lena. It was so unfortunate that she would not see Lili grow up. She had adored the little girl to distraction, and Lili loved her, too.

Stretching on tiptoes to place a kiss on his cheek, his mom added, "Thank you for giving me a second chance and allowing me to be a part of Lili's life."

Tyler positioned his hands on her shoulders and smiled down at her. "Mom, thank you, too, for cleaning up your act and coming to find me. Thank you for being there over the years. I can't tell you how wonderful it has been having you take care of Lili and me. It's been a blessing having you in our lives. And don't worry, Mom, we'll both pull through this difficult phase. I have painful memories here as well, but I believe we're meant to be here at this point. We'll help each other heal. I promise."

She smiled at her son and patted his cheek. "I love you."

"I love you, too, Mom."

* * *

"I'll see you tomorrow, Finn," Tyler said as he shook hands with his partner.

"Alright, Tyler." Finn walked to his car while Tyler nodded at the men trooping out of the building.

He just finished having a meeting with a crew of contractors along with Finn Tremblay at Anderson Realty. The project planned for the luxury mall was well underway.

Tyler swung into his car and drove through the busy streets of downtown Montreal. He glanced at his wristwatch and grimaced. He hoped he could make it in time to take Lili to her first dance class. Although his mom could always take her, he wanted to see Kaiya and straighten things out with her. Even though he wasn't looking forward to the meeting, it was something that needed to be done. He wouldn't have his daughter being treated differently if

Kaiya couldn't handle the past.

"Daddy!" Lili shouted as she walked down the spiral staircase with her grandmother in tow as soon as he opened the front door.

Tyler, with a bright smile on his face, walked toward his daughter, who hurried down the stairs and threw herself on him as she was wont to do whenever he came home.

The usual flush of emotions rushed through him as he enveloped her in a bear hug.

"Hello, Pumpkin. How was school today?" he asked and placed a kiss on her cheek.

Giggling, she replied, "It was fine, Daddy."

His eyes roamed her features, and pain squeezed his chest at how much Lili looked like her mother. They had the same color of hair and nose. He surmised that this was what her mother must have looked like at her age.

"What's wrong, Daddy?" Lili asked with worry in her voice and eyes that were just like his gray ones.

Reddening because he had been lost in thought while staring at his daughter, he kissed her cheek again and positioned her on the floor.

"Nothing's wrong, Pumpkin." His gaze lifted from her to his mother, who was also giving him a concerned frown.

"Hi Mom," he said, hoping to wipe the frown off her face with his gaiety.

"Hi, Ty. How did the meeting go?" she questioned, still giving him a queer look.

"Fine. Thanks for picking her up from school," he said, rubbing his daughter's dark dresses and smiling down at her.

"She has also had her lunch and is ready to go for her dance class," his mother replied.

Tyler already noted his daughter's baby pink tutu underneath her jacket. She looked so cute; he wanted to take a thousand pictures of her.

"Lunch is in the microwave in case you're hungry," she informed him as she stretched a hand toward her granddaughter.

"Er, Mom." Tyler ran his fingers through his midnight-black hair. "You don't have to bother yourself. I'll take her to the dance school."

The woman's brows arched.

"I want to have a word with the owner of the school."

After a moment's silence, she nodded. Tyler hoped she wouldn't take it to heart because she loved doing things with her granddaughter. He would have acquiesced, but he really wanted to be the one to take Lili to her first dance and every dance class, if possible.

She smiled and turned to the little girl. "Come give me a hug and a kiss, sweetie. Daddy is going to take you to your dance class."

"Okay, Grandma," Lili said and whirled her body to give the woman a hug and a kiss.

Tyler's mom kissed her granddaughter's cheek. "Have a nice time, sweetie. Remember, you're already a star."

Lili nodded and smiled. "Bye, Grandma."

"Bye, sweetie."

Tyler walked up to the imposing oaken front door with his daughter. He turned and nodded at his mother, who was observing both of them with fond eyes.

"See you later, Mom," he said as he opened the front door.

"Bye, Ty. Drive safely."

"I will, Mom," Tyler returned and shut the front door.

Hand in hand, father and daughter ambled to the car, where he helped her into the back seat. He helped her with her seatbelt, kissed her forehead, and shut the door.

Swiftly, he strode around the car and slid into the driver's seat. Through the rear-view mirror, he glanced at his daughter.

"Are you ready?"

She nodded.

Tyler acknowledged that the question was for him as much as it was for her. Was he ready to see that selfish woman again? He didn't think he was, but it couldn't be helped.

Chapter 3

A low sigh escaped from Tyler's lips as he pulled in front of Kaiya's dance studio, *Just Dance*. He stayed in that position for a moment looking at the large red building that was flagged by a restaurant and a spa. Tyler admitted that he would rather be at the dentist having his teeth pulled out than be there but for his daughter. He curved his body in his seat and gave Lili a tender smile.

"Here we are, Pumpkin. Do you think we should go in now, or do you want to wait till it's time to go in?"

Glancing around her as a car pulled to a stop beside theirs and a little girl climbed out of it with the aid of their mother, his daughter nodded.

"Let's go in, Daddy." Her voice was laced with excitement.

He wished he could be as enthusiastic as she was. Schooling his features, he pushed open the door and alighted from the vehicle. Quickly walking around the car, he reached his daughter's side and helped her with her seatbelt and also to alight from the car.

He held her hand as they walked into the cool interior of the building. Tyler pushed away the recollection of the other time he was there. Several pictures of girls in various dance positions graced the brown walls.

Intending to speak to Kaiya, he had come a little bit early. But now he was beginning to wonder if it wasn't a mistake because there was no one about. He glanced down at his daughter, who was looking around her with something akin to awe on her face.

Just then, a slim woman with blonde hair and a moon face walked into the lobby. She saw them and smiled broadly. Then she quickly walked over to them.

"Hello. I'm Molly," she introduced herself and shook hands with him after he told her his name. Then she bent to look at Lili. "And who's this pretty little angel?"

Giggling, his daughter answered, "I'm Lili."

"Well, it's nice to meet you, Lili. I'm Molly, one of the dance teachers here."

"It's nice to meet you, too, Miss Molly."

Smiling, the woman straightened. "I'm afraid you're a bit early. The lessons don't begin until the next twenty minutes."

Nodding, Tyler responded, "I know that. I'm here to see Ka...um, the owner of the dance studio." He didn't know whether she was still a Miss or had become a Mrs.

"Oh. That's a shame because she just stepped out."

Annoyance and relief poured through him. Why wasn't he looking forward to the confrontation with Kaiya? Perhaps it was because he was afraid that in his anger and disgust for her, he would say things that he could never take back.

The woman, obviously seeing the indecision in his eyes, remarked, "You can see her after the dance lessons."

When he hesitated, she glanced at Lili and back at him before adding, "You don't have to stay during the class. I assure you that Lili will be fine."

Tyler glanced down at his daughter, who smiled at him. Even though her eyes were as large as saucers— a tell-tale sign that she was nervous, she said, "You can go, Daddy. I'll be fine."

His brave little girl!

"Are you sure, Pumpkin?"

She nodded.

Tyler decided to leave. Perhaps it was good that he didn't need to stay since Lili would need to get acquainted with her fellow students and her teachers without him interfering.

"You can come back in an hour and half, Mr. Landry," Molly informed him.

He nodded then bent to give his daughter a hug and a kiss on her forehead. "I'll be back in time to pick you up, Pumpkin."

Lili nodded, then took the teacher's outstretched hand. Together, they left the lobby. His daughter turned and waved at him with a bright smile on her face.

He waved back even though he felt like scooping his daughter up and begging for her to remain his baby. It was just like her first day in school. The same thick bulge that had formed around his chest that day threatened to choke him now.

"She'll be fine," he whispered, struggling to reassure himself before turning around and leaving the building.

* * *

Kaiya's eyes misted for some seconds as they fell on the super cute kids who were introducing themselves. She didn't quite catch all their names because her mind had drifted to her late son. He would be their age had he lived. She was sure that he would have Tyler's gray eyes and his dark hair. Sometimes she wondered if her son would also have had a dimpled cheek like his father. Possibly he would have loved dancing.

Pushing such painful thoughts away from her mind, she focused on the 6-8 year old kids who were her favorites since they could easily communicate and were still very innocent.

She welcomed them again and walked them through the routine, "plie (plee-ay): to bend. Keeping both feet flat on the floor at all times, bend your knees. Releve (ruh-leh-vay): to rise. Saute (soh-tay): to jump)."

She smiled encouragingly at some of the kids who didn't get it. Some got it instantly, and she could see that they all liked it and were enjoying it.

Kaiya noticed a little girl who was quite good at following instructions. Although she seemed very shy, she was a fast learner. She caught on quickly whatever Kaiya was showing them. Completely impressed by the cute little girl, Kaiya called her forward and asked the other kids to be motivated by what she was doing.

The girl who she remembered was called Lili because she loved the name had dark curls, although her skin color was caramel— an indication that she had mixed heritage parents.

As the dance routine continued, Kaiya's eyes kept falling on the girl, and something nagged at her. Thinking about it for some minutes, she realized that the girl reminded her of someone. But who?

She continued showing the children the basics of ballet dancing, and when her eyes fell on Lili again, she froze. The little girl smiled, and then it hit her who Lili reminded her of.

Tyler!

But that couldn't be right. She shook her head. Not only had her nightmares returned, but now she was associating the jerk who had crushed her spirit with everything around her?

Damn him!

Focusing back on the dance steps, she showed her struggling students how to do them. The class finally came to an end, and everyone clapped. She praised her students and waited with them as their parents came to pick them one after the other. However, when after thirty minutes Lili's parents didn't come to pick her up, she grew worried.

Searching for her assistant, she asked her if she knew anything about Lili's parents. Shrugging, Molly told her that Lili's dad was the one who dropped her off. Gritting her teeth, Kaiya asked her to try contacting him. She couldn't wait to give the man a pep talk and remind him that this was not a daycare center.

Also, she wanted to get home soon since she had a new couch being delivered. Seeing the poor child seated all by herself, Kaiya retrieved a board game from a side table, and she walked up to her.

"Hello, Lili," she called as she sat on the floor with her, yoga style.

"Hi, Kaiya," the sweet child returned, looking down at her fingers.

Sensing how shy the girl was, Kaiya decided to draw her out by asking her questions as they played checkers. She found out her age and basic information about her. A pang hit her heart as she realized that Lili was the same age that her son would have been.

Lili loved the way the girl repeatedly giggled as they talked about all sorts of things and their favorite Disney princesses.

"I like snow white," Lili said, smiling down at the board.

"Oh, really? I think I prefer Rapunzel. When I was younger, I used to wish that I had hair as long as hers."

Lili giggled.

What a cutie! Kaiya thought. She so much enjoyed talking to the girl and playing checkers with her.

"I also love Ariel," Lili added quietly.

Kaiya shrugged. "I also used to wish I could sing like her." Then looking around conspiratorially and leaning in to draw closer to the child, she placed a finger across her lips. "Shh, don't tell anyone." She looked around her as if she didn't want anyone listening in. "I can't sing. I'll be paid not to sing if I dare open my mouth."

Throwing back her head, Lili engulfed in a fit of laughter. The sound was so beautiful that Kaiya just stared at her until she heard the door open and shut.

"Lili, I'm so sorry I'm late."

Freezing at the sound of the voice, Kaiya, in disbelief, turned around. Her eyes widened when she saw her handsome ex-boyfriend sauntering toward them with an apologetic smile on his face.

"Tyler?" Kaiya wanted to ask what he was doing there but paused. Then she put it together.

Lili was Tyler's child! The child he had with Lena. The child he left their child to be with and to raise. Her resentment bubbled at the surface as she pushed herself to her feet.

Icy eyes regarded him as he reached them and hugged his daughter.

"I was caught up in traffic, Pumpkin," he explained to the little girl who ran over to him and hugged his legs. He patted her hair.

Straightening, he presented Kaiya with a frosty stare of his own. Kaiya itched to slap his face. Of all the dance schools in Montreal, why had he chosen hers to register his daughter? Considering their history, she thought he would run a mile away from her. Why was the universe intent on punishing her?

"Sweetie, do you mind playing with the toys in the corner while I speak to your dad?"

She looked toward her dad, who nodded stiffly. Lili smiled and ran to the toys.

Folding her hands across her chest, Kaiya regarded Tyler with enough frostiness to freeze an erupting volcano. "Your daughter is beautiful. While I enjoyed her company, this isn't in any way a daycare."

Tyler's face tightened as his gray eyes became darker as he stared coldly at her. "Because God forbid you spend time with her," he said above a whisper. "You're right though, this isn't a daycare and you're nothing to my *daughter*. I was stuck in traffic and it won't happen again."

Seething as she registered his emphasis on the word 'daughter,' she almost yelled at him that he would have had a son, too, if he had lived. However, she controlled her emotions. It wouldn't do well of her to yell at the jerk while Lili wasn't too far from them.

"I don't think having your daughter at this school is a good idea. I can refer you to another one."

"No thanks," he bit back.

"Tyler, you don't understand. I..."

"No, you understand this. My daughter will remain at this school until her contract is up or until she decides, she doesn't like this school anymore. You will have to just deal with it," he said after cutting her off.

Keeping her cool, she stepped away from his hostile presence fearing she wouldn't be able to stop herself from hitting him continually while she asked him why he left. And why he is insistent of punishing her now. Since he insisted on keeping his child in her school, she would have to switch Lili to another class. She didn't think she'd be able to be around the girl knowing her own child died.

Smiling at Lili, she bade her goodbye and walked toward the door. The tension in the room was thick enough to cut with a knife, and it was beginning to give her a headache. If it wasn't for the fact that she handled the 6-8-year-olds and liked Lili, she would have told Molly to switch classes with her.

"Kaiya!"

The sound of her name halted her steps.

* * *

How could Kaiya be so heartless? She had another thing coming if she thought she was going to get rid of them that easily. She was the one who left him to deal with the consequences of their actions. With everything inside him, he wanted to ask her why he hadn't been good enough for her? Why she left him in the cruelest of ways?

However, he didn't think this was the time or the place to engage in such an emotional conversation. Struggling to ignore how beautiful she looked with her hair piled at the top of her head – although he always preferred her hair down and the leotard skimming her gorgeous body. He fought to recall why he had stopped her from leaving.

His teeth ground together inside his mouth when he registered that she was looking at him as if he were some pesky fly she was trying to get rid of.

"You'll be seeing my daughter often because we're here for the long haul."

Thrusting out her chin, she answered cuttingly. "Whatever."

"It would be very childish if you treat her differently based on our shared past. I also hope that my working with Finn won't cause interference from you either."

Throwing back her head, which gave him a full view of her lovely neck, she icily remarked, "You think I'd hurt a child just because their parent is an asshole?"

He shrugged and said, "Considering our past, I'll ignore that question."

"You must really pride yourself on having importance in my life. You mean absolutely nothing to me. You can go to hell for all I care."

Before Tyler could respond, she thrust open the door and all but slammed it in his face. Tyler clenched and unclenched his fists as he fought for control.

Thoughts of Kaiya consumed his mind as he drove home. He stopped to pick up some takeout for himself and Lili to take home as he had already told his mom not to bother with dinner. She had complained of a headache when he called her. He had told her to go to bed early.

He just stepped into the place when he almost bumped into Erin, an event planner he met a month ago at a luncheon they'd had with all the employees for the company he was working for. Erin was his colleague's sister, and she'd stopped by his workplace twice to visit her brother but made it a point to talk to Tyler.

On one of such visits, she had asked him out, but Tyler had ignored it since he had a daughter to raise and wasn't thinking about dating anyone anytime soon.

Tyler introduced Lili to the blonde-haired beauty with startling blue eyes and a great body. Erin fondly talked to the little girl. Seeing as Erin was there, Tyler decided they should eat at the restaurant instead of taking the food home. He asked Erin to join them, and she readily obliged.

As he observed how comfortable Lili was in Erin's presence and how the woman seemed to soak in everything Lili had to say as they ate, Tyler began having second thoughts. Maybe it would be nice to start thinking of dating again. It would be pleasant for Lili to have a mother figure again someday.

As the dinner progressed, Tyler got to know more about Erin, and he liked what he heard and saw. By the end of the meal, he acknowledged that he genuinely liked the woman.

Chapter 4

"Do you think Mom is going to be here before your due date?" Kaiya strolled into her kitchen the following day, clutching her phone in one hand and two bowls in her other hand. Sir and Lady, her Siamese cats purred around her feet.

"I have no idea. I still can't believe she took off just like that after promising me that she'd be there for my delivery," Kalilah said over the phone.

Kaiya chuckled as she poured a bottle of milk into the bowls she had placed on the kitchen island.

"She said she'd be back early," she commented as she placed one of the bowls on the floor for Lady while Sir eagerly waited for his. She smiled at him as she placed his own bowl of milk in front of him.

A heavy sigh from her sister got her brows arching. "Are you alright, Lah?"

"I'm fine. I'm just so exhausted these days. Between running around with Maximillian and Milania and work, I get very tired. Let's not even talk about my need to use the bathroom every thirty minutes."

Kaiya understood what her sister was talking about because she had experienced it all when she carried her son in her womb. A nostalgic feeling hit her. She could still remember the wonderful feeling of having her baby move, particularly at night when she couldn't sleep even when she was exhausted. And the full bladder that always had her running to the bathroom in order not to wet herself. There were also the weird cravings, the mood swings, and anticipation of the baby's arrival. But she never got to see the result and what it would have been like to have her baby in her arms.

Casting aside her thoughts, she encouraged her sister by telling her that it would soon be over and she would have her bundle of joy in her arms pretty soon. She quickly changed the topic by narrating to Kalilah her run-in with Tyler and his daughter.

"You know," she bit the inside of her cheek, "there's this part inside me that had always hoped that what Jalissa told me about Tyler having a child with Lena was untrue. But it's obviously true because I saw the proof in flesh and blood. A very cute proof if I must add."

Jealousy struck her again as she recalled that while Tyler and Lena were able to nurture their child, she had lost hers. For some minutes, she was overwhelmed once more at the loss of her child. Tears stung her eyes, and she hastily blinked them away.

Drawing in and letting out a deep breath, she continued, "And he had the guts to tell me that he hoped I wouldn't interfere with his business with Finn. I'm still confused about why he said that. Who your husband decides to work with is none of my business. You can tell him the unpleasant history between Tyler and me, but it wouldn't change anything. My son is still dead."

Kaiya chewed her bottom lip after her outburst. She hadn't meant to put Kalilah in an awkward position. Finally talking to someone about it was the reason for her outpouring of emotions.

"You know what I think you should do," her sister remarked after sighing. "I think you need proper closure."

"Closure?"

"Yes. You're obviously still very upset over what happened. It will do you a world of good if you confront Tyler so that you can finally move on."

A shiver of apprehension went through her at Kalilah's suggestion. The thought of talking to Tyler about their late baby filled her with so much uneasiness; beads of sweat marked her forehead.

"That's the only way you can move on, Yellow. Let him know how what he did affected you and hear what he has to say for himself."

"There is no excuse for what he did!" she retorted hotly.

"You'll never know until you confront him."

Biting her bottom lip, she sighed. "I'll think about it."

"Please do."

They discussed other things before Kalilah rang off. Kaiya had cereal for breakfast and prepared for her day ahead. Later, she was set to meet up with her ex booty call Marcus who is also her real estate agent. They needed to visit possible buildings for the other studio she was planning to open.

After viewing a few places with him, she ended things with Marcus. He was angry at first and asked her like a zillion times why she chose to break up with him. Kaiya had almost shouted that they didn't have anything going between them in the first place except sex. As if reading her mind, he asked if they could continue having sex and he would back off on asking her for a real relationship. She shook her head; she was done. Marcus finally accepted her decision and left the café a seemingly sad man.

In the afternoon, she hooked up with Jalissa, her best friend. They always had lunch together during the week. Her crazy friend had ridden to the restaurant as usual in her motorcycle. Their lunch topic had been all about Tyler, and Jalissa had enjoyed cussing him out.

The rest of the week was uneventful for Kaiya. She had school groups and meetings with prospective clients; she attended her private yoga classes and performed her arts and crafts activities as well as her DIY projects. She had taken up arts and crafts primarily after her son died to cope with losing him. It had helped her a great deal.

Kaiya also went to her women's support group, where she talked about her feelings which she couldn't share with anyone else on losing her child.

"So, Kaiya, you're up. How did your week go?" their leader asked as Kaiya took a sip from her glass of water, and her gaze fell on the other women seated in a circle around her.

"It went pretty well."

"Are you still having nightmares about your baby?"

She nodded. "But not so much. They began again because of the encounter I had with my ex. I can't believe he's back in town with his daughter from the woman he cheated on me with. I'm trying to look past it, but it hurts that her baby got to live, and mine didn't. I know such thoughts are negative, but I can't help it."

She paused and looked at the other women who regarded her with understanding.

"It's okay, Kaiya. Please continue."

Pushing back her tears because she needed to free her mind and this was the only place that she could without getting judged, she said, "Sometimes the guilt is so overwhelming. Perhaps she didn't wish her baby away the way I did when I found out that I was pregnant. If my dad hadn't had him cremated, I'm sure I would visit his grave every day to ask for his forgiveness. I know it might not be related, but I can't help feeling guilty that my baby died because he knew he wasn't wanted from the onset."

Tears streamed down her face as she stared at her hands with her head bent. The woman seated beside her placed a comforting hand on her shoulder.

"I still can't resist going into baby shops just to look around and wish things had turned out differently for me. I'm ashamed to say there are still times when I take his baby clothes out and sleep with them beside me.

When I see my nephew and niece, I can't help thinking about him and how much he would have loved playing with them. He would have been a handsome baby, and I regret that I never got to hold him, never got to kiss him, never got to tell him goodbye and tell him how much I loved him.

My sister is pregnant again and will soon give birth. I'm happy for her, indeed I am, but I can't help the jealousy that snakes up to my spine when I see her protruding stomach or hear her talk about things I went through when I was pregnant. I..."

Tears gushed out of her eyes as emotion clogged her throat. It was eight years, yet it still seemed like yesterday. Would she ever get past the knot in her heart? Would she ever come to terms with the fact that she lost a child, and she would never again have another? She promised her son, and she couldn't break that vow.

"It's alright, Kaiya. Take time to grieve for the loss of your child. I can't promise you that things with get better, but they do get easier over time. Time heals some wounds, but love heals all. The love you have for your son will help you move on from this. You're a beautiful young woman who deserves to be loved and to give love."

Kaiya nodded, even though she knew that she would never love anyone else again because she had chosen to love her baby forever.

* * *

The weeks flew by in a flash, and Kaiya had to admit to herself that she was slowly falling in love with Tyler's little girl. Lili never missed a session and her dedication to learning ballet made Kaiya delighted to have her in her class. She felt she was betraying her promise to her baby, but she couldn't help it. Lili was so adorable. Maybe the little girl was just what she needed to let go of her pain. She eventually changed her mind about switching the girl's class because she felt it would be unfair to the little girl who just wanted to learn how to dance. Besides, it would be unprofessional of her not to put aside her differences with the girl's father and give her the best.

One day, Kaiya was just stepping out of the building when Tyler dropped Lili off. She usually avoided being around when he dropped her off or picked her up so that they would have minimal contact with each other. Unfortunately, she had lost track of time that day.

Lili, after her dad helped her down the car, ran to embrace her; it warmed her heart. She patted the beautiful girl's head.

"How are you, Lili?"

Lili told her that she was doing okay and that she had gotten a new doll over the weekend. Kaiya suggested that she bring the doll to dance class with her so that she could see it, and Lili agreed.

Just then, Tyler walked up to them looking handsome in a pale blue polo shirt, black jeans, and black sneakers. His neck-length hair blew in the wind, causing it to fall unruly across his forehead.

"Kaiya," he said, nodding at her.

"Tyler," she simply said, avoiding looking at him as Lili rushed into the building.

Tyler stretched forth his hand to hand her his daughter's backpack. Their hands brushed, and time stood still for them. Sparks were ignited from the simple touch, and they stood there staring at each other in the sizzling tension. Kaiya wanted to deny that she didn't feel bolts shooting up her body as his hand met hers.

She tried to look away from his mesmerizing gray eyes which had turned darker, but it was an effort in vain. Thankfully, the arrival of a car in the parking lot broke the thick silence and highly charged moment.

With her color heightening, Kaiya nodded at Tyler and swiftly took the backpack inside, all the while asking herself what just happened.

She went to her office and sat there for some minutes to compose herself. Then she called herself a fool for reacting in such a manner.

"Of course, I'll react that way to him. We always had sparks flying between us, but that doesn't mean anything. He's still the loser who left me."

In control of her emotions again, she went to the dance studio and began her lessons. As usual, Lili was very attentive and was the best dancer in the class.

The dancers just finished the class when Jalissa, Kalilah, and Milania came into the studio. They exchanged pleasantries as parents picked up their children.

As usual, Tyler was tardy in coming to pick up Lili. Kaiya didn't mind; she was already used to it. Besides, since she was becoming fond of the little girl and enjoyed interacting with her, she had no complaints. She asked her niece to keep Lili company.

"Have you noticed that Lili has a resemblance to you?" Kalilah suddenly said into the conversation the three women were having.

Kaiya froze. "What?"

"Yeah," Jalissa concurred, staring intently at the little girl playing in the corner. "I see the resemblance. When I first saw her a few minutes ago, I was wondering who she reminded me of."

Kaiya gave an uneasy laugh because she had to talk about her rival. "Well, it's hardly surprising since back in the day a lot of people claimed Lena and I looked alike."

Gently chewing the inside of her cheeks, she recalled that the woman who

Tyler had cheated on her with also had the same dark hair, brown eyes, and heart-shaped face like her. Lili had those features which sprung up jealousy in her again.

Nodding with remembrance, Jalissa stated, "That's true. I remember, and I also remember how much it used to annoy you." She chuckled when Kaiya shot her a dirty look. "Well, it just went to show that Tyler had a type. Slim heart-shaped women with dark hair were obviously his thing."

"And Lili seems taken in with you," Kalilah pointed out. "She appears to be very comfortable with you."

Kaiya shrugged. She didn't mind having the girl around. Lili was a delight to be with.

Kaiya brushed past the two girls to get them glasses of juice as she did for every student whose parent was late in coming to pick them.

"My mommy is in heaven," Lili said to Milania at the play table where they were seated.

Kaiya's heart lurched and almost burst out of her chest at those words.

Oh, poor baby.

Kaiya had wondered several times where Lena was since she never showed up at the dance studio. She had wondered if the woman was miffed that her daughter was learning ballet in her rival's school.

Now that she knew the woman was deceased, she felt bad for Lili and Lena both. The woman had had a baby she couldn't nurture while she didn't have one. Kaiya bit her tongue from interjecting in the conversation and asking Lili what happened to her mother. For weeks, she had itched to ask Lili about her mother but always stopped herself just in time from snooping. Tyler wouldn't take it lightly if he found out she was questioning his daughter about their lives.

Just then, Tyler showed up with a petite blond older woman with a pixie haircut. Kaiya reckoned that at one time the woman would have been very beautiful. Although she still was, evidently, life had taken a toll on her.

Lili ran to them, calling, "Grandma." Kaiya was taken aback.

Grandma?

So, this was the woman who had engaged in so many alcoholic binges, that she neglected her son. Tyler must have sought her help when Lena passed away to help raise his daughter. Kaiya hoped the woman was sober now.

Kaiya grimaced inwardly at her unfair judgment of the woman. Tyler didn't look like the type of father who would allow his drunken mother near his child. She had to give him that even though he was a heartbreaker.

"Kaiya, this is my mother, Emelie," Tyler said when they reached her. "Mom, this is Kaiya Anderson, the owner of this place."

Apparently seeing her reaction when Lili ran up to them, the woman said, "I've been sober for ten years now, dear."

Flushed, Kaiya nodded. She was happy that Tyler now had his mom in his life. In the past, he had lamented a lot about her absence and worried about her constantly.

"Wait, did you just say Kaiya Anderson?"

Kaiya nodded and noted as the smile froze on the woman's face. Kaiya could visibly see as the woman recoiled from her and stepped away. She wanted to question the woman's reaction to her name but decided to ignore it. Instead, she dwelt on Tyler's dedication to his daughter.

The green-eyed monster reared its ugly head again as she wondered how he would've been with their child. She shook off the sad thought. Smiling brightly, she welcomed them. Jalissa, Kalilah, and Milania were also introduced to the woman, and they shook hands with her.

Thankfully, Lili chose that moment to say her goodbyes. She threw her arms around Kaiya's waist.

"Bye, Miss Kaiya."

As usual, touched by the gesture, she smiled at the little girl. "Bye, Lili. See you next time."

Turning to Milania, Lili said, "Would you like to come to my house for a play date?"

Milania nodded before turning to look at her mother. Plastering a dazzling smile on her face, Kalilah said, "Of course, she can come for a play date. In fact, her Aunt Kaiya will accompany her."

Kaiya let out an inaudible gasp and shot her sister the evil eye. Kalilah grinned and winked at her.

Turning, she stared at Tyler to see his reaction. His face was expressionless, but she could tell he wasn't pleased. Lili batted her eyelids at him, and her mouth formed a pout.

"Please, Daddy."

No one could resist such cuteness, especially as her mouth began wobbling; so Kaiya couldn't blame Tyler for grudgingly giving in.

"Okay, Pumpkin."

Lili and Milania whopped with delight. The little girl hugged her father and thanked him. She also hugged Kaiya and her newly-found playmate.

"What the heck was that?" Kaiya rounded on her sister the minute Lili and her guardians left.

"It's simply payback for the time you invited Finn to our girls night dinner years ago without my consent," Kalilah replied cheekily, placing her hand on her rotund stomach.

Kaiya groaned and wondered what she'd gotten herself entangled with. "But that was such a long time ago," she grumbled, biting the inside of her cheek.

Kalilah, in her glowing pregnancy look, laughed. "Revenge comes no matter how long it takes."

Kaiya rolled her eyes.

"Well, I don't think it's a good idea for Kaiya to be around Tyler. I don't trust him one bit," Jalissa said.

"Thank you!" Kaiya exclaimed, smiling at her best friend.

Kalilah giggled. "Too late! You're in trouble because I don't think this play date is gonna be just a Lili-Milania thing. Tyler will definitely be there. I noticed the undeniable sexual tension between you two."

Jalissa snickered. "I noticed that too. As a matter of fact, he looked at you lustfully several times when your attention was on Lili."

Kaiya threw up her hands in exasperation. "Oh, come on. Both of you are exaggerating. There's nothing going on between Tyler and me. I'd rather have something to do with the devil that that cheater."

Remorse filled her after her eruption. She hadn't meant to spoil the light and gaily mood. She just didn't want anything that would associate her with Tyler in that regard. Granted, there was still some chemistry between them—she was honest enough to admit that—but she was going to do absolutely nothing about it.

Apologizing to her sister and her friend who had been stunned into silence by her flare-up, she briskly walked away.

Chapter 5

Why the hell did I agree to this?

Tyler kept on asking himself that question as he tidied up the living room in preparation for Kaiya and her niece's visit. He wished now that he had found an excuse to escape from the so-called play date. But since he would do anything to make Lili happy, he had no choice.

And now he was going to have Kaiya in his home, and they were both going to pretend as if they didn't have a past between them. For a moment, he wondered if the children would notice the palpable tension that was always between them whenever they met. For their sakes, he was willing to put back his bitterness and play the cordial host.

As he stared around his still sparsely furnished living room, he wondered what she would think of the house. Would she think it was too ostentatious? Would she question why he had chosen to live there?

Staring out the window at the quiet street, Tyler saw Kaiya in his mind's eye. He couldn't get the image of her out of his thoughts.

She was more gorgeous than ever. From her jet-black hair to her beautiful face to her shapely body, Kaiya stirred something in him that he thought had died a long time ago.

Shaking off his thoughts, a frown marked his features. Beautiful though Kaiya might be, she had chosen not to be with him all those years ago. It was useless thinking of someone who didn't think he was worthy of being with her. He desperately needed to set those thoughts aside since she made her decision long ago, and she hadn't chosen him.

Nevertheless, he found it hard to stop his heart from hammering when thoughts of her flashed through his mind. He pondered on how it would have been between them had she not turned her back on him.

Glancing at the clock on the wall, he saw that it was only an hour before Kaiya and her niece would arrive. Hurrying, he arranged what little furniture the living room could boast of, made sure there was no single speck of dust in the room, and walked to the door.

The door opened before he could reach it, and his mother came into the room. From the look in her eyes, Tyler knew instinctively what she wanted to discuss. He had been avoiding the conversation ever since the day he introduced her to Kaiya at the dance school.

"Ty, I have something to discuss with you," she informed him as she walked toward one of the armchairs in the place.

Sighing inwardly, he followed her and stood by the fireplace, avoiding her gaze. She had obviously noticed him taking the extra time to clean himself up and the house to be in the best shape for Kaiya's arrival.

"What's going on between you and Kaiya?" she shot straight from the hip.

Wincing at the sharpness of her tone, he shook his head and said, "There's nothing going on between Kaiya and me." Feeling like a teenager who his mom had caught having sex, he reddened and ran his fingers through his hair.

Cocking her brows, she gave him a look packed with disbelief. "Are you sure? I saw the way the two of you looked at each other."

"Mom, please, believe me, nothing is going on between us. If anything, we can't stand each other."

She shook her head with doubt-filled eyes. "That wasn't the vibe I noticed the other day. And here you are, looking as if you stepped out of a man's magazine because you cleaned yourself up real good for today's meeting with her."

Blushing, Tyler looked at the shirt he had chosen to put on that day. He had a number of them he had never worn and had decided to put on one of them for the playdate. His chinos trousers were also creaseless, and his shoes were polished and shining.

"Tyler," his mom solemnly called, causing him to frown. Ignoring his reaction, she continued, "Is this woman going to pose a problem in our lives?"

Aghast that his mom would think that he would allow Kaiya in to break his heart again, he rubbed his hand across his face before saying, "Mom, I don't have any intention of bringing Kaiya into our lives. Our small family will stay as it is. And let me reiterate that there's nothing going on between us."

She clicked her tongue. "Could have fooled me."

Red-faced, Tyler looked away. From the corner of his eyes, he saw her rise from the chair. She walked slowly to him and placed a comforting hand on his shoulder.

"Sweetie, I don't want you to get hurt again. I don't want Lili to get hurt. All you've been doing these past days is cleaning the place just so that she can accept you. You want to show her that you're now equals, which is not necessary. You don't need her validation, Tyler. You're an amazing man, son, and father. Don't ever let anyone tell you otherwise."

Tyler just stood there, staring into thin air after his mom left. Had he been unconsciously trying to please Kaiya so that she would accept him in the same social status? That would be super foolish of him if that was what he had been doing. A faithless bitch didn't deserve any of it.

With a look of determination on his face, he took long strides to the door and yanked it open. The doorbell rang just then, and his heart slammed painfully against his chest. It was too late to go and undo all the things he had unconsciously done to please Kaiya.

He sighed heavily.

* * *

Kaiya wondered for the umpteenth time if she should have lied that she had a migraine or stomach upset just to get out of the play date. Kalilah, of course, would know she was faking it and would insist she went.

Why her sister couldn't understand that she felt like she was playing with the enemy was beyond her. When she picked up Milania, who was looking super cute in a pink dress, Kalilah had winked at her and told her to have a fabulous time.

Kaiya didn't think so because she knew that she would keep on recollecting past incidents when Tyler was around her.

The door opened, and her breath caught in her throat. Tyler was looking drop-dead gorgeous in a plain gray shirt which showed off his broad shoulders and masculine physique and black chinos trousers. Tyler looked so good and smelt so fresh and good that memories of their time together came rushing back. She remembered how good it was between them, and the bulge in her throat threatened to choke her.

Pushing it away, she said, "Hi."

"Hi yourself," Tyler replied in an unenthusiastic welcome. Then he gave the little girl standing beside her a dazzling smile that tugged at Kaiya's heart.

"Hello, Milania. Come on in."

Smiling shyly, Milania replied, "Hi Lili's daddy."

Tyler stepped aside for them to come in. Kaiya had been stunned when Tyler gave her his house address; where he resided was only for the rich, and now that she was seeing the size of the house with its impressive grand foyer, she marveled anew at how far Tyler had come. The teenager from group homes was now a wealthy man. Bitterness coursed through her as she acknowledged that this could have been theirs if he hadn't chosen Lena over her.

Schooling her features for the sake of the children, Kaiya followed Tyler to the living room. He then went to get his daughter who Kaiya was looking forward to seeing. Despite her animosity toward Lili's father, she adored the little girl.

Lili and Milania had their tea party while Tyler and Kaiya also participated. They drank tea and played board games with the children.

Since the children were such a delight to be with, Kaiya was glad that she had come to put smiles on their innocent faces. She was so happy that she wondered what it would feel like if they were a real family. What if Lili and Milania were their children, and they were all one big happy family?

Pushing away such unfruitful thoughts that would spoil her mood, she watched as the kids played together. Their sweet innocence touched her heart.

Kaiya noticed that Lili wasn't as shy as she first thought. The little girl was energetic. She carried on intelligent conversations that marveled Kaiya.

"You know what we should do? We should have a dance-off," Kaiya mentioned with a broad smile on her face.

"Yeah!" Lili and Milania chorused with excitement.

Tyler shook his head, but his daughter was having none of that. "Come on, Dad."

Tyler reluctantly agreed to join the dance-off, but he was soon smiling and enjoying himself. They danced to different genres. At the end of it, by unanimous vote, Kaiya was declared the winner.

"Thank you. Thank you." She bowed gracefully and smiled brightly. The two children clapped with excitement and giggled.

Suddenly, Tyler's eyes softened towards her, and he said, "Dance has always been your passion, and I can see that you're still very skilled."

Kaiya shifted uncomfortably at the compliment from Tyler. She didn't want him handing her compliments, yet she was touched by it at the same time. She looked away.

"Thank you," she muttered.

When it was time for them to leave, Lili pleaded with them to stay for dinner. Milania was very excited at the suggestion.

"I don't know. I'll have to call Kalilah to inform her of the change of plans."

Tyler, she noted, didn't say a word. His face was unreadable, which made her a little uneasy.

Kalilah, of course, said it was okay if they stayed over for dinner. Finn would come for his daughter later.

Dinner was a very lively affair. For the sake of the kids, Kaiya put aside her resentment and allowed herself to have a nice time. The lasagna meal was very tasty, and she had inquired as to who made the meal.

"My mom. Since being sober and becoming a grandmother, her obsession with cooking and baking has grown. Much to my delight of course. Lili and I both get home cooked meals and desert every day."

"Let her know that is lasagna is possibly the best I've eaten. Please don't tell Jalissa I said that."

"You secret is safe with me," he responded and then winked. Heat travelled through her body.

When dinner was over, Finn arrived to pick up Milania. The little girls hugged and waved each other goodbye. Kaiya decided it was her cue to leave as well. She turned to father and daughter with a genuine smile playing at her lips.

"Thank you for a wonderful time. I thoroughly enjoyed myself," she commented sweetly.

"You're welcome, Kaiya. We also had a wonderful time. Thank you for coming," Tyler returned with a smile on his face that she couldn't determine if it was genuine or not.

She turned to look at the little girl. "Thank you for inviting us for a play date. I'll see you when you come for classes, cutie."

"Kaiya, could you please read me a bedtime story?"

"Pumpkin, I don't think this is a good idea. Kaiya has to get home."

Chapter 6

Tyler tried in vain to stop the emotion coursing through him as he watched Kaiya read his daughter a bedtime story. He couldn't believe that he had allowed things to get this far. She didn't deserve to be there, but for the sake of his daughter, he had no choice but to accommodate it. He was a pushover when it came to his little princess. The lack of a mother in her life was already enough, he didn't want her to lack anything else. He gave in to most of her wants except one – getting her a cat. As he looked down at his ex and his child he couldn't help the feelings of contentment flowing through him as the woman who he used to love immensely tucked Lili into bed and placed a kiss on her forehead.

He nodded at her as she brushed past him into the hallway. Tyler walked to the bed and kissed his daughter on her forehead.

"Goodnight, Daddy."

"Goodnight, Pumpkin. Sleep tight."

He walked to the door, turned to tenderly smile at her before switching off the light and closing the door quietly.

Silently, he and Lili walked down the spiral staircase. For some reason he couldn't understand, he didn't want her to go just yet. He invited her to the living room for coffee. She reluctantly obliged.

Hurrying to the kitchen, he made the coffee, all the while asking himself what he was doing. It would be best for everyone concerned if he went to the living room and told her to go home. But since he had already invited her to stay, there was no going back.

He carried the mugs of coffee to the living room and saw that she had already settled down on the couch. He handed her the mug, careful their hands didn't touch. He didn't want any sensation running through him like when he had handed her Lili's backpack some days ago at the dance school.

Tyler pulled himself down on the couch beside her. They both sipped from their coffee without talking.

"Lili is a special child," Kaiya broke the silence. "She's so cute and smart."

He smiled the only way a parent would when his or her child was being talked about. "Indeed, she is," he concurred.

"You must be very proud of her," Kaiya continued shortly. "She's also a very good dancer. In fact, she's the best in her class."

Tyler had mixed reactions hearing that Lili loved to dance. He, however, didn't say anything but smiled.

"Once she sets her heart on doing something, she goes all the way, giving her best."

"Just like her father," she commented with a bright smile on her face.

He shrugged. He would have loved to tell her she got it from her mother, but he didn't want the conversation to become awkward. Although he still felt that she was nothing but a vain woman, he had to admit that he had had a nice time with her and Milania that day. Keeping his eyes and hands off her had been a great problem for him. Despite her betrayal, he couldn't keep his body from responding to her. She was gorgeous – still the most gorgeous woman he'd ever set eyes on.

"Why did you change your dream of becoming a professional ballerina into a dance teacher?"

He was surprised when he saw pain race across her face. Did she drop out due to failed exams, inability to cope, or something dark? Perhaps due to regret, remorse, self-recrimination, or what?

She shrugged and said, "Hopes and dreams change all the time. I didn't become a professional ballerina, but now I can help other little girls accomplish that dream if they want. There's this satisfaction I get when I see children who couldn't even take one step without feeling awkward end up dancing as if their lives depend on it; as if they were born dancing. I'm always teary-eyed when it's graduation day. I might not be doing what I desired to do when I was a teenager, but I'm happy with what I do now."

Tyler was sorry he had asked the question. He hadn't known that she would sound so defensive. What did she have to be defensive about anyway? She had made the choice. She had chosen...

Tyler mentally shook his head. This train of thought would only serve to get him infuriated. They had had a pleasant day, and he didn't want to spoil it by digging up the past.

"What about you? How did you end up owning your own business? According to Finn, you went to the university and are quite self-made with your real estate development company."

Was that jealousy he heard ringing in her voice, or was he mistaken? Why would she be jealous of him? It didn't make any sense.

"You asked about me?"

"I didn't, Kalilah asked while I was with them."

"After I moved to Vancouver, I enrolled into the university. I...er...I got a scholarship. I studied architecture, got a break, and started my own development company."

"I always thought you'd become a doctor. You were so good with science and math. I guess architecture is a good choice as well."

Was that bitterness he heard in her voice, or was he imagining things? Possibly he was, because he didn't think with her wealthy daddy behind her, ready to do whatever she desired, she wouldn't have everything at her beck and call. Had she thought that his life would go to shreds after she deserted him? It didn't matter to him though, as far as he was concerned, he got the better end of the trade. His amazing, smart, and well-adjusted daughter was proof of that.

Now, who sounds bitter? Shame washed through him.

"I guess...uh..." He didn't know what else to say. He had a lot of questions that he would like to ask her, but all of them would be dredging up the past.

"Do you still have a crush on Jude Law?"

The question apparently caught her off guard because she gave him a surprised laugh. "What?"

"Well, then, you thought he was the next best thing since sliced bread."

"Well, I think he is sexy!"

He rolled his eyes. "I bet you must have seen all his movies. I think his acting in King Arthur was mediocre at best. And don't get me started on Captain Marvel."

Kaiya looked appalled. "Kill yourself! His act was spectacular."

"Yeah, only a true fan would say that."

They argued about the actor, talked about some other blockbuster movies, and also about hit songs they favored back in the day and presently.

Before he knew it, an hour had gone, and they were still talking like long-lost friends. He recalled that in the past, they usually found it easy talking to each other. They could spend hours doing so and not get bored.

From the corner of his eye, he surveyed her glorious hair tumbling in waves across her shoulders. He loved it when she let her hair down and running free. It made her even more stunning.

Had he unconsciously moved or had they been sitting so closely together on the couch all evening?

Her nearness, her warm breath, and intoxicating fragrance, all triggered his senses. He turned slightly on the couch to scrutinize her. The way the dress clung to her breasts made him remember the one time they had been together and how he had caressed and worshiped the round molds.

The air thrummed with sexual tension. All Tyler could think of was carrying her off to his room, peeling that lovely blue dress off her body and burying himself so deep inside her; it would take a crane to pull him off. He adjusted himself uncomfortably on the couch.

Forgetting all the reasons why he shouldn't have anything to do with her, he leaned closer to her. Her lips parted, and it was all the invitation he needed. He brushed his lips against hers. She was hesitant at first, but a second later, she pulled his shirt and delved into the kiss.

The kiss went on and on as their tongues danced in a rhythm as old as time. Tyler's hand rose to delve into her hair, drawing her closer to increase the intensity of the kiss.

A loan moan from her got him jerking back to his senses. It took a great deal of effort, but he was able to wrench his lips from hers. Her swollen lips and her dazed eyes made him long to place his lips on hers again, but he controlled himself.

Frowning thickly, he snapped, "That was a mistake. We shouldn't do it again."

With her face flushed, she cleared her throat, nodded, and said. "I agree."

An awkward blanket of silence fell between them.

"It's late," he curtly said and rose. "You should get going."

Avoiding his gaze, she rose swiftly.

He couldn't believe that after everything that happened in the past, he allowed himself to be taken in by her beauty and intoxicating presence. Why couldn't he stop the helpless yearning he felt to be one with her again?

After falling hopelessly in love with her, at first sight, all those years ago and going into a relationship with her, he never thought that they would one day part ways, and in such a bitter manner.

Over the years, she had haunted his dreams although he, as good as, hated her for what she did. When she was sixteen years old, she had captivated him. But now, the twenty-five-year-old woman had him completely mesmerized to his chagrin.

Even as he was mad at her for coming into his life again and stirring up the sexual emotions in him, he still ached to draw her into his arms and satiate himself into her again.

Standing there with her eyes dazed with sexual passion, Tyler could see that if he pressed, she was his for the taking. Perhaps if they had sex, they could get the sexual tension brimming between them out of the way and move forward.

He shook his head inwardly. Once wouldn't be enough for him. It would only serve to increase his longing for her. She was like a drug to his senses that he would have to take over and over again. And before he knew it, he would be a slave to her every whim again.

With just one afternoon spent in her intoxicating presence, he had thrown away the years of pain she had caused him. Tyler gritted his teeth at his stupidity. Even though she was all grown now, she was still the same woman on the inside.

He could never make the mistake of hooking up with her again. Never!

* * *

Stung by Tyler's icy tone, Kaiya wondered what had gone wrong. A minute ago, he was kissing her as if she was the only woman in the world, devouring her lips as if he would never let go. And now he was staring at her with icy contempt.

Her lips still tingled from his kisses, and her whole body had become awake from his touch. She had never felt this way before, not with Marcus.

What a kiss! What an explosive kiss! It was nothing at all like the first kiss they had shared, which she had thought was magical then. This was certainly volcanic in comparison.

Self-consciously, she walked to the door and thrust it open, aware that Tyler was walking behind her. Her thoughts were all over the place as she walked through the foyer.

"Are you going to the Gala next weekend?" Their family's annual charity gala was coming up, and since he now worked with Finn, he was probably given an invite.

"I'm not sure yet. I probably won't attend, to be honest. You?"

"I have never missed one, and I don't intend to this year."

Wasn't it insane of her to want him to kiss her again and again till he never stopped? Her body was hot and tingling from the effect of the devastating kiss. It was just like that night together in the park when she had lost every sense of reasoning after he kissed her. All she could think of was him moving inside her, which was exactly how she felt now.

Twin red spots stained her cheeks at her erotic thoughts. Even after so many years, she still lusted after Tyler's body. What a shame!

Shaking off the effect of the drugging kiss, she tried to bring back the resentment she had for him. Even though they shared chemistry that could light up the whole of Montreal, it didn't change the fact that he had chosen Lena over her and abandoned her when she was pregnant with his baby.

The kiss, the chemistry between them, the urge to have him make love to her had to be forgotten because he was still a jerk.

Besides, she felt as if she was breaking the promise she had made to her deceased son a long time ago. She had promised not to love anyone else; to keep his memory fresh forever in her mind and never to let anyone else in.

Unfortunately, she was beginning to lose focus of that resolve simply because she met Tyler again. As a teenager, she had been enamored by Tyler, unable to stop thinking about him even when they were right beside each other.

The feeling that she was being sucked into Tyler's web again plagued her. He had been sweetness itself all day until a few minutes ago when he turned to Ice Man.

For the umpteenth time, Kaiya wondered about the animosity she usually sensed in him. What did he have to be angry about? She was the injured party here who was still finding it hard to forgive him for what he did to her. Possibly if their son had lived, she might have been able to accept him. But she hadn't even told him about their son.

Did he have to know? Not that it would change anything. She was certain that he would come up with a flimsy excuse to explain what happened years ago. She wasn't in the mood to listen to lies.

"Thanks once more for a wonderful evening." She turned when she got to the front door.

For a moment, she wondered if he wasn't going to respond. He just stood there looking at her with an unreadable expression and his hands in his trouser pockets.

"Thank you, too," he simply replied.

As Kayla whirled around to open the door, she knew she wouldn't be back here, ever. It was best if they stayed away from each other.

Climbing into her black BMW M240i Cabriolet, Kaiya acknowledged that while she had had a spectacular day with Tyler and the kids, it had ended in disaster. She should never have stayed back, and she should never have allowed him to kiss her. Now he probably thought she was all hot for him. Even if she was, he didn't need to know.

Angry with herself that she couldn't control her emotions where Tyler was concerned, she turned the key in the ignition, revved up the engine, and drove away as if the hounds of Hades were after her.

Chapter 7

Classic music sounded in the hall where the Anderson Realty Gala was being held. Kaiya, taking in the gay atmosphere, decided she would love to be someplace else, probably at home, trying to sculpt something. But since she was an Anderson, she had to be in attendance.

She sipped from her champagne and looked around at the Anderson employees and friends who were having a nice time. Some were dancing to the music and generally having fun.

Kaiya wished she could share in their enthusiasm instead of struggling to push Tyler from her thoughts.

It was a week since the play date and the devastating kiss between her and Tyler. She hadn't set eyes on him since that night when she left his house. It was a deliberate act, she suspected, and she welcomed it. A distance between them was best for both of them. Their history was too painful for them to be in each other's company all the time. Frayed nerves were set to go off, and the results would surely be unpleasant.

Since she, too, had been very busy trying to finalize the deal on her new school, she didn't mind the fact that he no longer dropped off and picked Lili at the dance school.

His mom did all that now, and although the woman treated her frostily, it hadn't stopped Kaiya from being warm and friendly to her. At least she got to see Lili every day, which was a blessing. Her bond with the little girl was growing, and Kaiya was beginning to fear that her strained relationship with the beautiful girl's father might affect her connection with Lili.

What if Tyler suddenly decided that he didn't want his daughter coming to her dance school anymore? What would she do then? Would she give up on the little girl or try to work on her relationship with Tyler?

She would be devastated if she didn't get to see Lili every day. She wouldn't worry about it now. Enjoying this party was what she would try to do.

Seeing her mom who just returned from her trip to Europe, she weaved her way through the crowd to reach her. Her sister wasn't in attendance because she wasn't feeling well.

Unfortunately, her mom couldn't talk much because she kept being called away, or their conversation was interrupted by someone or a couple who wanted to say hello.

Giving up, Kaiya mixed with the crowd, having conversations with some of the people she had known almost all her life.

"Hello, beautiful."

Kaiya turned to see Marcus looking splendid in a tux. A low groan left her throat. She had forgotten that he was a part of her Finn's staff.

Smiling stiffly, she replied, "Marcus! You look good."

"Not as good as you," he answered, his gaze sensually going down her body that was clad in a strapless black sequin dress that ended just below her knees.

"Thank you," she responded with a smile that didn't reach her eyes.

Smiling seductively, Marcus said, "Can I have this dance?"

Reluctantly, she nodded and took his outstretched hand. On the dance floor, she protested a little when Marcus drew her so close to his body that she couldn't breathe. He apologized and stepped away a little.

"I've missed you terribly, Kaiya," he commented as they moved their body to the rhythm of the music.

She didn't say anything. What was there to say? She hadn't even thought of him to forget missing him. Maybe it had something to do with the fact that she wanted a man who she considered her enemy to make love to her.

"Please reconsider our relationship. My body burns for you." He drew her close again, and Kaiya gasped when she felt the throbbing bulge poking below her stomach. She blushed and looked around her. Shamelessly, Marcus continued. "Feel what you do to me, Kaiya. The mere sight of you drives me crazy. We should be together."

"It was just sex, nothing more," she inserted coolly.

With a harsh whisper, he refuted her statement. "No, it's not just sex. We're made for each other."

Kaiya rolled her eyes just as the hairs at the back of her neck stood. For some reason, she felt she was being watched intently by someone. But when her gaze trailed the room, she couldn't find the suspect. Everyone was doing their thing.

Kaiya gritted her teeth and hoped the song would end soon because she couldn't take Marcus's sensual words anymore nor his blatant arousal still poking at her body.

A low sigh of relief fell from her mouth when the dance finally came to an end. Marcus asked for another, but she politely refused.

Shaking her head, she remarked, "Please excuse me. I have to use the washroom."

She noticed Marcus was following her only when she had reached the end of the hall. She decided to ignore him. She reached the washroom and gave him a pointed stare to deter him from coming in with her. To her amazement, he did.

"What do you want, Marcus?" she queried sharply, folding her hands across her chest.

"You know you want me, Kaiya," he purred, covering the distance between them.

"Not anymore." She eyed him angrily. "Now, please leave, I need to use the washroom."

"Do you really want me to leave?" His eyes dimmed, which annoyed her further.

"Please leave, Marcus."

The breath burst out of her chest when he dragged her into his arms.

"I'll leave after I get what I want!" he threatened ominously, causing a shiver of trepidation to go up to her spine.

* * *

Tyler didn't know what compelled him to, but he decided to follow Kaiya. He had seethed at a corner as he watched her dance with that other man.

He had just arrived at the gala, which was a last-minute decision on his part, and found Kaiya in the crowd immediately but in the arms of another man who she seemed more than a little acquainted with. He had gritted his teeth all through as he observed the way the man's hands had moved all over her body as he danced with her. If he was asked for his opinion, he wouldn't have called it dancing; he would have called it caressing while moving. Although her face hadn't seemed as if she was enjoying it, he had expected her to pull away when the man drew her so close that there wasn't any space in between them.

His eyes narrowed when he saw the man follow Kaiya out of the hall. Irritated, he also noticed the tell-tale bulge in the man's trousers. He felt like smashing the man's face as he watched the man leave the hall. It was obvious what they were going to do.

Tyler was stunned that he was feeling this way. It was none of his business if Kaiya and the man were going to have sex in the washroom or wherever they were heading. Her sex life was none of his business. Even though he ached to slake his lust in her delectable body, it didn't mean he was actually going to do it.

For two weeks, thoughts of her had tormented his every being. And he had questioned more than ever the choice she made all those years ago. He had decided it was best if he avoided her, but he hadn't been able to stop himself from coming this evening, even if it was just to get a glance of her from a distance. However, he hadn't envisaged that he would watch her in the arms of another man.

When he saw that Kaiya was frowning at the man and not smiling at him, which he assumed she wouldn't do if they were going to have sex, he knew he had read the situation incorrectly. And so, he followed them out of the hall.

He got to the washroom just in time to see Kaiya struggling with the man and yelling at him to get his hands off of her. Incensed that the man was trying to take liberties with her that was unwelcomed, he reached for him, whirled him around, and punched him in the gut. The man doubled over, but that didn't stop Tyler from punching his face.

"Tyler, stop!" Kaiya shouted.

He grabbed the man by the neck. "Don't you ever come near Kaiya again if you know what's good for you!"

The man nodded, and Tyler pushed him to the door and threw him out of the washroom.

"I didn't—"

He cut off whatever she was about to say when he slammed the bathroom door shut and locked it.

Eyeing her intently as he breathed in and out heavily, he rasped, "Why do I always have to rescue you from lustful males?"

Seemingly affronted by his words, she folded her arms across her chest and dealt him with a stare filled with anger.

"I didn't need your help then, and I didn't need it just now. I had the situation under control," she retorted hotly.

Shocked laughter left his throat at her ingratitude

"Indeed, you had. Who is he, and what's your relationship with him?"

"That's none of your business!"

Seeing her looking so flushed yet so beautiful with her hair falling across her shoulders. Recalling the first time they met all those years ago triggered something in him that made him reach for her. He dragged her into his arms and fastened his hot lips on hers.

He half-expected her to pull away and grace his face with a slap, but she instead wrapped herself around him. That was all the encouragement he needed to deepen the kiss. He stroked his tongue across her lips as her fingers pushed into his hair, massaging his head. A low moan escaped from her lips as she drew her head back, and he trailed kisses along her lovely neck.

Reaching around for the zip at the back of her dress, he drew it down and freed her breasts from the clinging material. He had itched to do that when he saw her in the sexy little dress. When her perfect, well-rounded breasts thrust into his face after he pulled the dress away, he nearly wept for joy. They were bigger now.

His hot lips explored the rosy peaks, which had become rock hard pebbles. Kaiya whimpered when he sucked them to perfection. He kept at it for some minutes while she made stimulating moans in her throat.

When his manhood, which had become as hard as steel, became too painful to ignore, he reluctantly released her breasts and reached under the dress for her panties.

With one quick swipe, he tore the lacy material off her waist, and his fingers found the hot, moist core of her. Maddeningly, he explored her folds as she arched her back, and he could see sensations running through her face.

"Please," she begged breathlessly, and her hands went to his belt. He continued exploring her clit as she unbuckled his belt and drew down his zipper. Tyler's hand stilled when she clutched his manhood after she pulled down his boxers.

Lifting her, he deposited her on the vanity and spread her legs apart. Without wasting any more time since he felt as if he would die if he wasn't inside her in the next second, he positioned his manhood in the entrance of her core and slowly slid in.

Her core was drenched, slicking a smooth passage until he was buried deep within, but only for a moment. He pulled out until only his tip remained in her. She whimpered at the loss, but he slammed back, driving her body backward with the force of his movement.

The movement of his hips increased as he slid into her repeatedly. Lost in a frenzy of passion he hadn't experienced in a long while, he pounded mercilessly into her, totally oblivious of their surroundings as she moaned with pleasure.

His mouth claimed hers as she reached her peak while he went on thrusting in and out of her for a while before his body convulsed with sensations as old as time itself. With a guttural groan, he let go of himself and enjoyed the tumultuous feelings that poured out of him. His hot seed spilled unrestrained into her as spasms kept on rippling through him in one of his most explosive orgasms ever.

Just as he had feared that day on his couch a week ago, one taste of Kaiya wouldn't be enough. Already, he wanted her again.

Shit!

* * *

The realization of what she had just done with Tyler hit Kaiya when he slowly pulled out of her. Immediately he stepped away from her, she quickly drew her dress up, avoiding his gaze.

Kaiya couldn't believe that she had just had sex with Tyler considering there was a room full of people a few feet away. And to make it worse, she wanted to do it all over again. Her face reddened as she recalled the expert way he just brought her to fulfillment. If she was being sincere with herself, he was the best she ever had. Right from their first time together till now, years later.

He must have gained a wealth of experience over the years. Resentment pulsed through her as she remembered that while he was having sex with her, he was also doing the same with Lena.

Thank God she didn't get anything from him. Well, except her son.

The euphoria of the moment came crashing down to be replaced by icy derision. She remembered how much he had hurt her.

"That was a mistake," she said into the awkward silence that had fallen between them as they struggled to steady their breaths. "I can't believe I allowed you to have sex with me when you're nothing but a liar!"

Tyler jerked his head back as if she had struck him. His eyes narrowed. "A liar? What did I ever lie to you about?"

Seeing that her panties were ruined, she threw them in the bin and curled her lip at him.

"You told me that you and Lena were just friends; housemates," she threw at him with a savage bite. "When you were, in fact, lovers. You were sleeping with both of us and couldn't be man enough to admit it. Coward!"

Looking stunned, Tyler's lips tightened. "I don't know what you're talking about. If there's any coward here, it's you!"

Aghast, she stared at him with fury. "Coward? How dare you call me a coward, you no-good, lying, two-timing piece of shit."

Tyler's face became as hard as a rock. "You can call me whatever you want. It doesn't hide the fact that you left me and threw away everything we created without giving us a chance."

"Left you?" Kaiya almost reached out to claw his eyes out for daring to throw that accusation her way. He was indeed a liar! Trying to save face when confronted with the truth.

She opened her mouth to cuss him out when her phone buzzed inside her clutch. Ignoring him, she took the clutch from the ground where it had dropped when he shoved her into the washroom and opened it.

Kaiya clutched at her chest as she read the text that just came in. It was from her mom. Kalilah was in labor. She returned the phone back to the clutch and gave him a glare packed with contempt.

"While I would love to continue this conversation, to show you how much of a lair you are, I've got to go."

"What's wrong?"

She heard the reluctance in the question, and she bit the inside of her cheek, wondering if she should tell him what was going on since it was none of his business. Surmising that he wouldn't let her go until she told him as he was blocking the entrance, she acquiesced.

"Kalilah is in labor. I'm heading to the hospital right now," she informed him perfunctorily.

"What hospital is she in?"

Her brows went up. "What business of it is yours?

Grimacing, he said, "You've changed."

Those words warmed her more than anything he had said or done since he came back to Montreal. What did he expect? That she would become all putty in his arms, forget about his betrayal? Her color heightened when she remembered that she had indeed become putty in his hands a short while ago, and had, in fact, begged him to make love to her. Frostily, she replied, "You just never knew me." Then she told him the name of the hospital.

He stepped aside as she brushed past him, grateful to be away from his intoxicating presence. She quickly redid her makeup before dashing out of the place as if it was on fire.

Outside the hall, she took in large gulps of air, trying to steady her nerves before she drove to the hospital. As she slid into the cool interior of the car, she realized that Tyler didn't use any protection, and she had just gotten off the pill since she broke things with Marcus.

Shit!

Chapter 8

K alilah's third child – Myles, was beautiful, and Finn was right beside his wife, comforting her and whispering words of encouragement in her ears on what an amazing job she did.

He kissed her repeatedly and called her sweet names. Powerless to stop it, Kaiya felt slightly jealous of the couple and their newborn son.

Unable to control her thoughts, she began to wonder what life would have been like if her baby survived. If Tyler had been by her side when she was giving birth, would things have turned out differently?

Her mom looked at her sympathetically, probably sensing her sadness. The woman would know what she was going through at the moment because she had been there through it all. Instead of Tyler to be by her side holding her hand, it had been her mom who stood in for him. Her mom had murmured words of encouragement at her and told her how beautiful and strong she was.

Oh, the pain had been unbearable. At such a young age, she had never experienced something so painful in all her life. Her mom, gripping her hand, had told her that she could do it, she could push out her baby. But if she couldn't, she could always go through a cesarean section. Afraid of going under the knife, Kaiya had put in her all and pushed out her baby. Unfortunately, she had lost a lot of blood, which had all the doctors and nurses running helter-skelter to salvage the situation. Too weak to even open her eyes, she had slept off only to wake up and be told that her baby hadn't made it.

Holding back the tears, Kaiya excused herself from the room.

* * *

What am I doing here?

Tyler questioned himself continually. He was hiding under the guise that he was here to offer support to Kaiya when, in fact, it wasn't needed. The baby had been born, and according to the nurse he asked, mother and son were doing just fine.

So why was he really here hanging around the deserted hallway? For some reason he couldn't understand, he felt he needed to be there.

Tyler was still thinking and trying to make sense of the argument he had with Kaiya right after they had sex. It was odd that all their time, they hadn't talked about their child, and it'd been burning Tyler to not say anything to Kaiya. He kept on waiting for Kaiya to say something about it, but she said nothing.

Was she that heartless? How could she not even care about them?

Suddenly, the woman occupying his thoughts stormed out of the room, crying.

"Kaiya!" Tyler called after her, but she ignored him.

Tyler noted that she was furious. He could tell by the tension in her shoulders. It wouldn't be surprising if she had had an argument with her father concerning him even at such a euphoric moment. The man was a kill-joy. He hurried to where she was, and grabbed her hand, whirling her around.

Kaiya, with tears streaming down her face, raised her hand and struck him hard across the face. Tyler's head jerked back as he held his stinging cheek.

"What the hell was that for?"

"How could you?" she queried cuttingly, looking like an avenging angel with narrowed eyes, flaring nose, and tightened lips.

Tyler had no idea what she was talking about, but as she continued to cry brokenly, he took her hand. She hesitated at first, but when he was persistent, she reluctantly allowed him to drag her back to the waiting room. Thankfully no one was sitting in the room that late in the night. The TV was on, but it was muted.

Rounding on him on the chair with fiery eyes, Kaiya all but yelled at him, "How could you have cheated on me with Lena? How could you have gotten her pregnant and moved away with her? And you did all these while I was pregnant with your son! You left me all alone and to grieve alone. How could you?"

Cheated on her? Son? What in the world was she talking about?

Tyler was rendered incapable of any coherent thought as he studied her crying brokenly. Her head was bent, and her shoulders shook with the sobs wracking her body.

Lifting her head and staring into her eyes that were consumed by pent-up pain, he hoarsely said, "I swear to you that I never cheated on you!"

Wrenching her face from his hands, she shouted, "Stop lying! Your daughter is proof that you cheated on me! You chose Lena."

A thick knot formed in his throat, as he was still trying to decipher what she was saying. It was all very confusing to him.

"Please tell me about this son of ours you're talking about."

Sniffing, she narrated her story, "I discovered that I was pregnant two weeks after that night at the park. I was so scared; I didn't know what to do. All I knew was that I had to tell you immediately. I kept on trying your number and sending texts, but you never replied to any. For months, I kept trying to reach you without any response from you. I had never felt so alone in my life."

The image of her being holed up in her room crying her eyes out and feeling all alone because she couldn't reach him tormented him to his soul. He let go of that feeling wanting to hear the remainder of the story. He didn't want to feel sorry for her after what she did.

"My parents eventually found out." She shivered involuntarily. He understood that she just recalled the scenario when they found out. His face blanched at the harsh words that must have been spoken to her, mainly by her father.

"They whisked me away to New Brunswick to give birth and hide me from the shame that was bound to befall them from their snobbish social circle."

That explained a few things.

"I waited and waited for you to come or contact me, but you never did. On the day of the delivery, I was in so much pain, that nothing the doctors gave me seemed to work. I found it hard to push since I was in so much pain, but I eventually did." She smiled through the tears gushing down her face. "I was very weak when I pushed him out of my body, but I heard the faint sound of his cries until the doctor whisked our son away, saying there's a complication. I wanted to hold him. I begged and cried to hold him believing that if he were in my arms, he would be fine. But I was so weak because I had lost so much blood, I passed out." Sniffing, she went on, apparently oblivious that all the color had drained from his face. "I woke up two days later and was told by my mom that I'd lost my son and that Dad had him cremated, believing that if I saw my dead son, I'd never recover."

Interesting.

"I never got to hold him, never got to tell him how much I loved him. I was depressed for a full year after. I somehow blamed myself; I still do. I felt that if I had loved him enough, he wouldn't have died. If I had wanted him from the first time I discovered I was pregnant instead of wishing him away, he would still be alive today. I killed our son. I'm so sorry." Her sobs were louder now, and it broke his heart and not for the first time to understand how truly wicked her father was.

"It took me a long time to come to terms with the death of our son, but till now, I still suffer anxiety attacks, mostly when I'm with babies. Eventually, I picked up the pieces of my life and forged ahead, but his memory has never been far from my thoughts."

He didn't know what to make of everything she told him. She seemed genuine enough, but it seemed almost unbelievable. Her story explained the animosity she felt for him. And if everything she told him was true, then she was about to go through a world of hurt when she learned his side of the story.

"Kaiya," he began gently, struggling to put the words together without calling her a liar, "I'm finding it extremely hard to believe all the things you've just said."

Disbelief flashed in her eyes. "Are you calling me a liar?"

"No, I'm just saying that your story will sound more credible if I see *my son's* death certificate."

Kaiya's jaw dropped.

* * *

For the life of her, Kaiya couldn't believe that after pouring out the ordeal she went through to Tyler, he didn't believe her. As a matter of fact, he all but called her a liar.

Glaring at him as she itched to slap his face again, she saw her dad walk into the room from the corner of her eye. Dabbing at her eyes with the handkerchief Tyler offered her, she walked up to the man.

Richard eyed her warily. And then his eyes became consumed with fury, and she guessed that Tyler was behind her.

"Dad, I'd like to see my son's death certificate."

"What?" All the color drained from his face.

Sniffing, she went on, "I want to show Tyler our son's death certificate. You..." Her tongue dashed across her lips. "You handled everything, didn't you?"

Throwing Tyler a death stare, Richard replied, "I did."

"Then I'd like to see it." It had been too painful for her at that time to look at it, and over the years, she hadn't felt the compulsion to. But now, she wanted to look at it. She had no idea what her father had named her son. Too weak to even stay conscious, she hadn't even thought of a name for her baby.

The recollection of the whole painful incident was threatening to do her in, but she kept strong. Tears had been shed repeatedly for many years, but she wanted more than that now. She needed closure.

"I thought I told you to stay away from him." Kaiya's father's mouth had formed a grim line as he stared behind her with revulsion.

Exasperated, Kaiya's snapped, "Dad, this has nothing to do with staying away from Tyler or not. It was his son, too. Now, I need you to show him the death certificate because he thinks I'm lying about having a baby."

Shrugging, he announced in-between clenched teeth, "You don't owe him anything."

"Dad, please, I need my son's death certificate."

"I can't do that."

Caught off guard by his response, she could only blink at him as her lips parted.

"Er...why?" she finally asked when she could find her voice. Her dad was still staring at Tyler like something he would like to squash underneath his expensive shoe.

"I was on my way to the airport before you stopped me. I'm leaving for a business meeting. When I get back, you'll get the damned certificate!"

Not liking her father's words yet incapable of doing anything about it, she watched as he briskly walked away from them, his nostrils flaring and flattened lips.

Kaiya turned to Tyler to assure him he would get the certificate as soon as her dad returned from his business trip. The words died in her throat when she caught him studying her with an expression she couldn't decipher.

"I've got to go," he hastily said, and before she could say anything, he brushed past her.

Standing there feeling all alone again, she questioned what just happened. Tyler had never appeared intimidated by her dad. But now she wondered if the men had had a silent exchange that she knew nothing about. Was that the reason for Tyler's hasty departure?

All the thinking and weeping was giving her a headache. She settled herself on one of the chairs in the waiting area and curled up there.

She jerked on the chair when she went over the whole incident that just happened and registered that Tyler hadn't seemed surprised when she mentioned that she had gotten pregnant. He was more interested in his dead son. What was going on here? Had he somehow found out that she had gotten pregnant? Was that why he stayed away? Did he know about their son dying before now? Suddenly, nothing made sense anymore.

* * *

"Richard," Tyler called to the man who was striding purposefully to his car in the hospital's parking lot.

Kaiya's father whirled around, and his face tightened with fury. "What do you want, you lowlife? Didn't I warn you to stay away from my daughter? How dare you come back to Montreal? How dare you show your face here?"

Tyler reached him and glared at him as if he was something unpleasant that he just threw up.

"How could you do something so terrible to your own child? You're despicable!" Tyler told him squarely.

Richard's face reddened with a contemptuous stare, but he thrust out his chin at the man glaring at him. "You think you're so smart, don't you? You think you can come back here and turn my daughter against me, don't you?" He let out a harsh bark of laughter. "By the time I'm done with you, you'll leave Montreal so fast; you won't have time to shake the dust off your shoes."

Tyler's face darkened with rage. With frosty calm, he said, "Don't you think it's a little too late for such threats?"

The older man's fists folded and said with total conviction, "Empty threats, you say. You better watch your back. And I better not see you at any of our functions anymore."

"I didn't come here to exchange words with you." He dipped his hand into his jacket pocket and brought out a check. "Here's the money you gave me to stay out of your daughter's life." He thrust it into the man's stiff hand. "It was the sole reason I went to the gala tonight. You can rest easy knowing that you will never see me in any of your functions anymore."

Staring at the piece of paper as if it were some sort of UFO, the man tore the check into shreds. Then he lifted his head and stared at Tyler with daggers in his eyes. He stonily stated, "If you know what's good for you, stay away from my daughter. She deserves better."

"You're right, she deserves better than you." Tyler said then began to walk away and then stopped. "Oh and Richard, I'm giving you the courtesy of telling your daughter the truth. If you don't, I will. You have two weeks." With everything that he learned tonight, he knew the next few weeks for him and Kaiya would be tough. If his father was anything like Kaiya's, he was glad he didn't know the man. The unpleasant encounter with the despicable man left him in distaste. He couldn't wait to get home and cuddle his daughter in his arms, promising to never do such an inhumane thing to his darling Lili.

Chapter 9

Two weeks later...

There was much gaiety and laughter in the large living room. The entire Anderson and Tremblay families, along with their friends, were all gathered in Finn and Kalilah's house for Myles' baptism. There was much to eat and drink thanks to Jalissa's catering services. Everyone was having a good time. The baby kept being passed from one hand to the other.

It eventually got to Kaiya's turn, and she was super pleased to cuddle her newborn nephew in her arms. She forced thoughts of her son who she never got to cuddle away from her mind.

She lifted her head and searched for her best friend in the room. She wanted to ask Jalissa if she had gotten a piece of the action. If she hadn't, then she could take a few minutes cuddling the baby. Jalissa loved babies but was adamant about not having any herself. They often joked that they'd end up being the cat ladies when they're older.

Her eyes narrowed when she saw Justin hand Jalissa a drink before taking a seat on the couch next to her. The suspicion that Finn's brother had a thing for her best friend flowed within her. She didn't know if she liked it. They were both grown, but Kaiya knew her best friend. She never did relationships. Her longest relationship thus far was her friendship with Kaiya. She never dated a man for longer than ninety days. She hoped Justin wasn't looking for anything serious.

Jalissa caught her eye, whispered something to Justin before rising from the chair.

Without pulling any punches, Kaiya asked, "What's going on between you and Justin?"

Mouth agape, Jalissa eyed her. "What makes you think something is going on between us?"

"Uh, I've got eyes."

Her best friend giggled. "It's nothing serious, Kai. Just a harmless flirtation."

"Harmless or not, do you think it's appropriate?"

"Oh, Kai, stop being a wet blanket. It's just sex, nothing serious."

"Are you sure?"

Jalissa let out a groan and rolled her eyes. "He's sticking it into me, and I'm enjoying it for now. That's all. We're both going to get bored with it soon and then we'll move on. End of story."

Although not satisfied with her friend's explanation, Kaiya nodded and said, "Well, I hope you know what you're doing."

"Stop being a worrywart."

"I don't want either of you getting hurt."

"Alright, Mama."

Kaiya gave her friend a look which made her burst into laughter. She quickly ended it in order not to wake the baby.

As the twins started crying, Justin went over to tend to them. Jalissa followed him soon after, which caused Kaiya's brows to rise.

Her concentration, however, shifted to her parents when they excused themselves from the living room and headed for Finn's office. She believed her father had been avoiding her, much like Tyler has. It had been two weeks since she last saw Tyler and Lili, and she missed Lili. Tyler had called the school to inform them that Lili would be visiting with her aunt for two weeks and wouldn't be able to attend classes. *It was probably a lie,* she reasoned. She needed to get her child's death certificate from her father to prove to Tyler that she isn't a liar. She handed the baby over to his father and followed her parents to Finn's study.

"Where's my son's death certificate, Dad?"

Her parents seemed taken aback as she entered the office without making any form of noise.

"I told you you'd get it. I returned from my trip only yesterday," her dad snapped, avoiding her gaze as he paced to the window.

Before Kaiya could demand that they go home immediately so he could hand it over to her, Kalilah and Finn entered the office.

"All of you disappeared in there. What's going on?" Kalilah asked with a worried frown on her face.

"Nothing," Richard hastily answered. "Finn, I must say that your mall is—"

"Oh, please, Richard. For God's sake, tell your daughter the truth!" Her mom cried. "I'm tired of being a part of this lie!"

Alarm bells rang in Kaiya's brain even as all the color washed off her face. *Lies?*

"Mom, what are you talking about?" Her voice came out as a squeal.

"Richard!" the woman snapped instead of answering her.

With her teeth almost biting a huge chunk from the insides of her cheek, Kaiya observed with a shiver running up to her spine as her father slowly turned from the window. In a matter of seconds, he seemed to have aged drastically. His face was drawn, and there were lines of strain on his forehead. He avoided looking at anyone in the room, contented with staring at the floor.

"Oh, alright! I'm sick and tired of it, too, particularly since that bastard came back here. I can't believe it, even after I told him to stay away from Kaiya!"

Kaiya nervously dashed the tip of her tongue across her parched lips. She was afraid that if her heartbeat became faster than how it already was, her heart would jump out of her chest.

And the whole story came out. The truth about what happened eight years ago poured out from her dad's taut lips.

They had sent Kaiya away to New Brunswick in a boarding school for pregnant teens so that their friends wouldn't find out about the pregnancy.

"What else?" She already knew that, and it had taken her a while to forgive them for it.

Richard paid off doctors in the New Brunswick clinic to pretend that her baby was a boy and then to say he passed away. Richard then took her baby daughter and gave her up for adoption.

The words exploded in Kaiya's brain. *No!* She denied it. *It couldn't be true.* Her father couldn't have been so callous as to do this to her and watch her grieve for years. Her fingers bit into her palm as she fought for control.

The shock had her knees quivering as she recalled the night of the delivery, and the moment her mother told her that her baby had returned to God. All these years, she had mourned a baby who was still alive and was a she instead of a he. Hot tears cascaded down her cheeks as pain squeezed her chest. Was she sure that these two strangers had indeed birthed her?

"I can't believe it. Who did you give my baby to? Oh my God, you gave away your own grandchild to strangers!" she shouted, too shocked to formulate any thoughts.

"Not to strangers," her mom responded, seemingly shamefaced with tears in her eyes, but her daughter wasn't moved by it.

"Then, who?"

"I gave the child to her father," her father simply said.

Her father?

Tyler was her baby's father. That would mean that her father gave her baby to Tyler. That would mean that...

The room began to spin. Her hand reached out to grab the handle of the armchair to keep her steady, but it came in contact with the air. As there was nothing to hold her back, she welcomed the darkness that enveloped her.

She came to a few minutes later, clearly disoriented but very weak. Her eyes roamed around the room as she wondered what was going on. Then it all came back to her, crashing into her brain like an avalanche. Her father had given her baby away for adoption to the baby's own father.

Fury at the man who she called a father washed through her. All those years of pain, regret, anguish, sorrow had been a waste of time because her child was alive and well.

"How could you do this to her, Father? This was the same way you manipulated Finn and me! Is there no end to this?" Kalilah, who was seated beside her on the couch and holding her hand, shouted at their father. Kaiya slowly pushed herself to a sitting position.

"I did what I thought was best for her."

"Tell her the rest," Katherine silently ordered her husband.

Sighing, the man finished recounting past events. He ended the story by telling them he gave Tyler a 2-million-dollar check so he could care for the baby. He asked Tyler to stay away from Kaiya. He didn't have the guts to send his only grandchild to a family he didn't know, and so he lied to Tyler and told him Kaiya wasn't interested in raising the child and wanted to pursue her dance career more than motherhood.

Kaiya thought that she had recovered, but when the room began spinning again, she slowly laid down on the couch. Her mind went through all her father just said, and she understood Tyler's initial animosity toward her. He believed that she had chosen her career over motherhood, over being a family with him and their daughter. Now she understood why he had been shocked that first day at the studio and asked why she didn't follow her dream of becoming a professional ballet dancer. He had been fed with lies, horrid lies by a man that she would hate till her dying day.

Her eyes fell on her mother who was seated huddled on a chair and looking forlorn, but Kaiya felt no pity for her. She had been part of the whole charade, and so she didn't deserve any.

"And you, Mom, you stood by and watched Dad perpetrate such an evil act against me?" She threw at the woman with a savage bite as she again pushed herself into a sitting position.

The woman paled – her eyes glazed with tears.

"I didn't know anything about it. Your father kept it from me. I found out soon after Kalilah and Finn's accident, hence the animosity and separation between us. Why do you think I took off to Europe? When I saw Tyler, I knew that your father's lies would be brought to light."

Her niece and nephew were born eight months after her sister's car accident and would soon be five years old, which means that... "You knew for almost five years, and you didn't tell me? Mother, you knew how much I suffered after the loss of my child."

"Please, Kaiya. I didn't know how to tell you. When I found out, I was in shock myself, and I wanted to tell you, but you had just started putting your life back together. I didn't want to stop your progress."

"Finding out that my child was alive would have done nothing to stop my progress! If anything, my grief would go away. But you should have told me! You should have confessed what he did before now!" Kaiya yelled at her. "He had no right to give away my child! You were aware of how depressed I felt about losing my child and the man I loved. For years you watched me grieve without saying a word. If Tyler hadn't returned and asked for his son's death certificate, you would have allowed me to stay in the dark forever. Kalilah was right about you two. You are monsters!"

Her mother jerked on the chair, grief-stricken.

"Kaiya, I won't accept your insolence toward your mother!"

Kaiya turned at the sharp reprimand of her name to her father who was standing by the window and giving her a stern look.

"Fuck what you accept! You took my child from me!" She had never spoken to her father with such disrespect and it felt freeing. She was always on eggshells when he was near.

"Watch how you talk to me! Whatever was done was for your own good. You had your life ahead of you. With a baby and a gold-digging bastard in tow, you would never have amounted to this much in life."

Kaiya's jaw dropped. She couldn't believe her ears. Her father was trying to justify destroying her life.

"It was my decision to make, not yours. And do you call this a life?" Living in sorrow, living in misery over the supposed death of her baby, and thinking the boy she loved betrayed and left her for another woman and their child?

How's that supposed to be the life? Little wonder she hadn't found closure. She mourned for a child – a son that never existed in the first place.

"I hate you!" She turned to glare at her silently weeping mother. "I hate you both! You might as well forget that you have me as a daughter!"

"Forget you have any children," she heard Kalilah say as she jerked up from the chair she sat on and quickly stormed out of the room. Not bothering with her jacket, she left the house through the backdoor. Her hands were clasped around her midriff as the autumn breeze blew around her. How Tyler must have hated her all these years thinking she gave up on him and their baby. No wonder he said that night at the gala that she hadn't trusted him enough. All the pain and anguish they had both felt over the years washed through her. All the animosity they had felt for each other was all for nothing.

She desperately needed to see him. She had to ask for his forgiveness on behalf of herself and her wicked father. She had hated him all these years for nothing.

* * *

When Tyler opened his door to a disheveled Kaiya with red and puffy eyes, he already knew what she was going to say before she opened her mouth.

"I never gave up our daughter!" she whispered in a broken voice.

Tyler, with a grim face, knew immediately that her father told her the truth. He opened the door wider and stepped aside for her to come in.

After his conversation with Richard at the hospital, he had put together the truth and was waiting on Richard to tell Kaiya the truth. If he hadn't, Tyler had planned to confront him about the truth in Kaiya's presence. The contemptible man had deceived both him and Kaiya. How a man could be so contemptible was beyond him. What amazed him was the fact that Richard still felt justified by what he did to him and Kaiya. He hadn't sensed any remorse in the older man that night. Instead, he had been full of threats.

"I swear, I didn't know all that happened. I found out only a few minutes ago," she sniffed as tears poured down her already wet face. "How could my father have done such a callous thing to me? He knows how I suffered all these years. He's aware of how I couldn't let go of the memory of my supposed late son. He—"

Her voice broke as she sobbed heavily. At a loss for words and feeling like crying himself, Tyler bent a little and swung her into his arms. He couldn't watch her cry so brokenly.

Up the stairs he went with her. He crossed the landing and took her to his room. All the while, sobs still wracked her body. He murmured words of sympathy and encouragement to her, but she cried heedlessly.

Tyler laid her on the king-sized bed and held her until her sobs began to subside. She needed to cry it out, so he didn't stop her. He only provided the comfort he knew that she desperately needed.

His thoughts drifted to when she talked about their deceased son at the hospital. He had struggled to believe her, but he eventually did. For the past two weeks after realizing that Kaiya might be in the dark about what her father did, he knew he would need to tell Lili the truth. Now that Kaiya had finally found out the truth, he didn't know how to go about it. The thick lump in his throat threatened to choke him.

"Is Lili home?" Kaiya questioned in a small voice after she put a hold on her flailing emotions.

He shook his head. "No."

He was thankful that Lili was hanging out with his mom today since she didn't need to hear the things that would need to be discussed.

When a companionable silence passed through them for some minutes, Tyler decided that it was time for her to hear his own side of the story.

"Are you up for hearing what happened from my own side?" he questioned softly.

She nodded, still holding him tautly.

Sighing, his mind drifted back to years ago when he had been nothing but a naïve teenager. But he knew better now.

"Remember that last night we overslept at the hotel? The educator on shift had my phone confiscated, and I got grounded. Later that morning, I got into a fight with another boy at the group home because of some nasty things he said about you. It wasn't a pretty sight. It was so bad that we were sent to a youth detention center for a few months. By the time I came out of the detention center, I had turned 18. I looked for you everywhere, but I heard that you'd left Montreal to attend school in another province. I was devastated. I tried to find out the actual place where you were so that I could come to see you, but no one knew."

He remembered how sad he was when he searched for her and nothing came up.

"Lena, who had also turned eighteen, came to my rescue. She talked some sense into me about at least trying to become somebody so that when I found you again, I wouldn't still be the riffraff that you once knew. I picked myself up. Since we'd turned eighteen, it meant that we couldn't stay in the group home anymore. We found a tiny apartment and got work at a fast-food joint."

He continued the story by telling her about the night where he had two visitors that would change the trajectory of his life. The first visit was from his mother who claimed to be sober. He was apprehensive to see again. She hadn't come to be part of his life again; she just wanted to tell him that she had been sober for two years. He was just happy to hear that she didn't drink anymore. Another knock on the apartment door revealed Richard with a car seat that held a tiny baby. In the coldest manner ever, he gave Tyler the check, the application for Lili's birth certificate with Kaiya's signature, and he told Tyler that Kaiya had given birth to his daughter. He told Tyler that Kaiya had relinquished all parental rights to the baby and didn't want it since she got accepted to join a professional ballet company. One look at the baby girl and he knew that she was his daughter.

"He walked away after warning me to stay away from you. Although I was nervous yet happy to have a daughter, I was shattered that you didn't want our baby. For hours, I just looked at the baby and wept that her mother didn't want her and had chosen her career over her."

"I didn't, Ty, I swear, I didn't know. I will never forgive them. They stole my daughter's childhood from me."

"I was so distraught that I wanted to go and find you to beg you not to give up on us and our baby. I wanted to tell you that being with me and our daughter would never stop you from achieving your dream."

Lena and his mom had stopped him because they'd heard Kaiya's father threaten bodily harm and arrest if he ever came near her again.

He wanted to return the money, but his mom and Lena advised him not to look a gift horse in the mouth. He needed the money to take care of his daughter. He planned to give it back to Richard somehow, though; he had way more wealth now.

He decided that he would go to college and make something of himself for his daughter's sake. He wanted her to regret her decision when she saw how successful he would be and how beautiful and wonderful their daughter turned out to be.

"Some days later, Lena came up with the suggestion of leaving Montreal for someplace else to get a new start. We decided to leave for British Columbia for a fresh start since it's warmer there."

"I wish you came to find me. I wish..." Her voice trailed off as she took a deep breath.

Kaiya burst into tears suddenly. He understood how she felt. All these years, they had both hated each other, thinking they were abandoned by the other. He wished he could punch Richard's face for causing them so much pain. Instead, he cuddled her closer and told her everything would be fine.

Chapter 10

For a long time, Kaiya couldn't stop herself from weeping. She laid in Tyler's arms on the bed and allowed the discoveries of the day wash over her. She still couldn't wrap her head around how devious and conniving her father had been. And to think he claimed he had done it for her own good. Granted, she loved the fact that she was a ballet teacher and had her own school and hoped to set up more, but her life would have been more fulfilled. Having her daughter and Tyler by her side would have made her life extremely happier than how it could have been.

Sighing ruefully, she shook her head. For years, she had blamed herself for her baby's death. She had thought she was being punished for getting pregnant and wishing her baby away. She had also faced insecurities that she might never have another baby because of the fear of losing it again.

All these she had discussed with her women's support group, but she couldn't really say it had helped because she still found herself going to baby shops to stare at and inhale baby things, longing for her baby. Subconsciously she still celebrated her baby's birthday every year, lighting a candle and buying a cake, even if it was a cupcake.

"Are you alright?" Tyler asked beside her.

It was evening now. They had remained lying on the bed, talking about everything that happened.

"I still can't believe that I have a daughter and not a son. A daughter that is very much alive," she delivered after a few minutes.

"With time, you will. I'm here for you Kai," Tyler stated quietly.

"Please, tell me about Lili. Other than the fact that she's super cute, smart, and a great dancer, I don't know anything about her." Those words saddened her and brought tears to her eyes, which she hastily pushed away.

Tyler caressed her hair in comfort. "I'll tell you everything you need to know about her." Then he gently pulled her from his body. He rose and stretched a hand toward her. "Come with me."

"Where?" She eyed him with curiosity.

"To the living room. I want to show you everything you need to know about your daughter."

Nodding, she pushed herself off the bed and took his hand. Together, hand in hand, they walked down the spiral staircase. Although her heart was beating rapidly against her chest, Kaiya applauded Tyler on the beauty and opulence of the house. He shrugged it off.

In the living room, Tyler opened a cupboard and brought out a box. He directed her to sit on the couch and placed the box on her lap. Kaiya bit her bottom lip as she stared uneasily at the box that would tell her things about her daughter.

"Go on," he urged quietly and sat beside her.

With her heart beating against her chest and her hand shaking a little, she lifted the box's lid. There were pictures, albums, and DVDs inside the box.

Tears glazed her eyes as she looked at numerous pictures of her daughter during her growing years. There were so many of them that it took a while going through it all. Her heart squeezed with pain as she saw every milestone she missed. Her daughter's first smile, her first words, her first steps, her first day in school. She missed everything!

Pain tugged at her heart. How could the ache in her soul ever go away when her daughter had learned to call another woman, 'Mom' while she was still alive?

Jealousy snaked up her body as she saw Lena in a lot of the pictures.

"Lena seems to be in a lot of the pictures," she couldn't help commenting.

As if hearing the jealousy in her voice, Tyler looked at her queerly. "Lena was a good mother figure to Lili."

Was she a good wife to you? Kaiya wondered. *Did she fill the gap that my absence caused? Did she love you the way I loved you?*

Kaiya mentally shook those painful thoughts from her mind and focused on the pictures. Lena seemed to have really loved Lili. Tears flowed down her cheeks as she realized everything she missed. Another woman had shown her daughter the love she would have given her had she been aware of her existence.

"I'm sorry if it's going to bring back painful memories, but I overheard Lili telling Milania that her mother was in heaven. What happened to her?"

Kaiya dug her fingers into her palm to keep her jealousy from showing when she saw the intense sadness that crossed Tyler's face.

"A drunk driver rammed into the rear of her car when she was coming back home one evening. Lili was in the car, but thankfully she wasn't harmed. Unfortunately, Lena lost her life in the accident."

"I'm sorry to hear that. How devastated you must have been."

He nodded with sorrow in his eyes. "Indeed, I was."

"She must have meant a lot to you," she stated, fishing for words on how involved they were.

Noncommittally, Tyler remarked, "She was a good friend and mother figure to Lili." His voice cracked.

Sensing that he wasn't going to say anything more about the deceased woman, she asked, "Why did you name her Lili?"

An affectionate smile crossed his face and he quickly excused himself from the living room and returned with some documents in his hand and handed them to her. She looked down and saw it was a birth certificate issued from New Brunswick.

"Her full name is Kyla Liliana Landry."

"You combined our names."

"Lena did actually. We were thinking of a name for this precious baby girl and Lena suggested Kyla jokingly, but I agreed immediately. My mom liked Anna and I liked Lily, so we combined the two."

It was so sweet of him to have still wanted to name a part of their daughter after her, even though he thought she had abandoned her baby. A sob caught in her throat.

His arm went around her. "Even though I hated you for leaving us, I was grateful that you gave me such a precious gift. I was so happy that you didn't terminate, or worse, given her to strangers."

She shook her head. "I would never do that to my baby, even if its father was the devil himself."

She looked down at the birth certificate and saw that her name was indeed listed as Lili's mom. This threw her off. She asked Tyler about that.

"When your dad handed me our daughter, he said that you'd already signed the birth record and named me as the father. He said that only my signature was missing to make it official. I signed it quickly and gave it back to him so that he could hand over to the officials in New Brunswick. It was easy for me to apply for her birth certificate after that."

More tears pooled her eyes. She remembered signing some documents after she'd been told that her son had died. Her father had said that it was documents for the death certificate. She was so out of it, given the fact that sedatives had been administered to her after she learned that her child had died. She had never bothered to read anything she signed. Why would she, she trusted her father. Trusted that he had her best interests at heart.

"I thought I was signing my son's death declaration and cremation forms. How could they do this to me. Their own child. I could never do that to..."

"Shhh, I know babe. It's gonna be okay." Kaiya took solace in Tyler's arms, enjoying the warmth his body produced.

Lifting her head and gazing into his eyes, she said, "Thank you for giving her a part of me. My name."

He smiled and brushed a loose strand of hair from her forehead. "She has more than your name; she has your spirit." She was touched by his words.

After that, things became easier to talk about. He told her how challenging his life had been raising a newborn while he attended University. Even though he had help in the persons of his mom and Lena, he had still desired to spend a lot of time with his daughter. He had changed her diapers, fed her, and rocked her to sleep.

His words made Kaiya more depressed about everything she missed. Her hatred for her father grew.

I'll never forgive him, she resolved inwardly.

* * *

"You can't imagine the horror I felt the day she came up to me and told me that she wanted to become a professional ballet dancer. All I could think was that she was indeed her mother's daughter!"

Kaiya laughed heartily.

Tyler watched as Kaiya's brown eyes brightened as she laughed. He was glad that the tears had dried up in her eyes as they spent the past two hours trying to catch up from the time they'd been apart to the present. They had also talked of ways they would present the news of her being Lili's real mother to the little girl.

With Lili spending the weekend with his mom at his mom's sister's house, he and Kaiya had had the whole house to themselves talking and watching videos of their daughter.

For hours, he had itched to draw her into his arms and kiss her passionately, but he controlled himself. The memory of their hot sex in the washroom was still fresh on his mind. He wanted to take things slowly with her this time around. He would worship her glorious body with kisses before he made her his yet again.

As if she sensed what he was thinking, she whirled her body to his on the couch. Perhaps she saw the desire in his eyes for her lips parted, and her eyes became glazed.

Reaching out, he caught a strand of her hair, caressed it, and then ever so slowly, he covered the distance between them.

Tyler cradled her face and brushed his lips against hers. His mouth left her lips moments later and worshiped her beautiful face with kisses. His lips covered hers again, as his tongue stroked hers.

His hands went from her face and lowered to her breasts. He kneaded them while Kaiya moaned with pleasure. The kiss wasn't broken even as his hands roamed and caressed her body.

94

Their tongues locked as they continued smooching on the couch. Kaiya reached for the buttons of his shirt as his hand went behind her shift dress to lower the zip.

When his lips closed on her nipple through her dress, she arched her back, and he felt the sensations running through her body. His body shook from nearly uncontrollable desire.

He had promised himself that he would take things slowly this time around, but he was afraid that he wouldn't be able to keep that promise because he wanted her so badly, he couldn't wait. Perhaps after taking her fast and hard, then he could go slowly. After all, they had all night to make love since both his mom and Lili wouldn't be back tonight.

Tyler removed his hands and mouth from Kaiya's body and was just about to rise so that he could carry her back upstairs to his room when the doorbell rang.

They both froze.

Tyler wondered who in the world could have such poor timing. He gritted his teeth as he rose from the chair.

Kaiya giggled. "Perhaps you should do something about that before answering the door."

Tyler followed the direction of her sultry gaze and hot pink stained his cheeks. He took her advice and breathed in and out slowly even as the doorbell sounded again.

Fully in control of his emotions and making his manhood placid again, he briskly walked across the foyer to the front door.

He froze for the second time in minutes when he saw Erin, looking lovely in a cream and red off-shoulder dress, standing there.

Shit! He had forgotten he had a date with her.

"You didn't forget about our date, did you?"

Raking his fingers in his hair, he shook his head and fibbed. "Of course not. Please come in."

He stepped aside for her to enter. She marveled at the interior of the house and told him how beautiful it was. He thanked her and led the way to the living room, hoping that Kaiya had made herself presentable.

Shit!

The astonishment in Kaiya's eyes when they walked into the room spoke volumes. Gracefully, she curved her body in their direction. Erin paused by the door, and he could see the shock and question in her eyes as well.

"Kaiya, this is Erin. Erin, this is Kaiya," he introduced without placing any title on both women.

Both women exchanged pleasantries, but he noted that it was stilted. An awkward silence fell in the room after he showed Erin to a chair.

"It's getting late. I better get going," Kaiya announced as she swiftly rose to her feet. "Thanks for everything, Tyler. I'll call you tomorrow."

Tyler wanted to tell her not to leave, but he couldn't since he had to go out on a date with Erin.

Rising also, he replied, "I'll see you to the door."

She waved a nonchalant hand at him. "Oh, don't bother. You have a visitor." Then turning to the said visitor, she presented her with a bright smile. "It was nice meeting you, Erin."

"It was nice meeting you, too, Kaiya," Erin returned with a forced smile of her own.

Tyler could see that Kaiya was disappointed.

He ignored her request to not walk her to the door and followed her. She didn't say a word to him as they crossed the foyer. He opened his mouth to tell her that he would schedule a time when they could tell Lili the truth, but he closed it tautly when, without sparing him a glance, Kaiya opened the door and quietly shut it behind her.

Tyler wished he could go after her, but he didn't. Erin was waiting for him, and he owed her an apology. He knew one thing for sure, he couldn't put stock into dating anyone at the moment. His daughter would need him more than ever right now – Kaiya too.

Chapter 11

E*rin!*

Kaiya couldn't wrap her mind around the fact that Tyler was dating someone.

Frowning, she knew she had no reason to be upset since they weren't in a relationship. But that didn't take the hurt away. He was dating another woman, and he might marry her. And then Lili would have a stepmom, yet another mom who wasn't her. Erin seemed nice, but who was to say that she would treat Lili nicely. She needed to stop thinking so negatively.

Exhausted from the trying events of the day, Kaiya pulled her car into her driveway and just sat there for some minutes, going over the happenings.

If she ever saw her parents again, it would be too soon. She never wanted to set eyes on them ever again. Even though her mom had nothing to do with the deception, she would at least have confided in her daughter when she found out what her husband did. If Tyler hadn't come into the picture and demanded for a death certificate, her mom would have continued to keep it from her.

Exhaling softly, she let herself out of the car and trudged to her door. She unlocked it, pushed it open, and strode to her living room.

A sharp gasp fell from her lips when she saw her sister cuddled on her new couch with her baby.

"Kalilah?"

"Oh, thank God you're back, Kaiya. I've been so worried about you." Kalilah set the baby down on the couch and immediately came over to hug her. "I've been trying to reach you for hours. You switched off your phone."

"I needed time to talk things out with Tyler."

"I figured that you were with him, so I decided to come here and wait."

"Thank you."

Kaiya and her sister walked to the couch. Kaiya carried the baby and sat while her sister curled her body beside her.

"How could they have done such a thing to me, Lah?"

Her sister sighed loudly. "Sometimes, I wonder what planet they're from because they're so heartless."

"You can say that again."

She and Kalilah talked at length about everything involving their parents.

"I am never going to speak to him again," Kaiya said furiously.

"Me either. Finn gave it to Dad fiercely."

"The gall of it all is that he feels justified with what he did. He feels no remorse whatsoever. He never even apologized."

"Let's not talk about him anymore because it's getting me upset all over again. I'll like to talk about my niece. After my anger passed, I was so excited that I had a niece. I'm so glad that your child is alive."

"Me too. Even though I spent years mourning a nonexistent son, I'm so glad that Lili is my daughter."

Kaiya spent the next thirty minutes talking about her daughter and every-thing Tyler told her about the little girl. Kalilah listened with tears in her eyes. It was obvious that she was very happy for her sister.

"Speaking about Tyler, do you know he's dating someone?"

"No way!"

Kaiya sadly nodded. "Yes, he is. I met her. She came over to the house. I think they're going out on a date or something."

Kalilah reached out and caressed her hand.

"It's okay. I don't expect that we'll get back together because we have a daughter."

"Everything will be fine, Kaiya. Work on your relationship with your daughter first, then see how things go with Tyler," Kalilah added quietly.

Smiling with tears in her eyes, Kaiya said, "Thanks, Lah."

* * *

Tyler trudged down the stairs to kitchen where his mom was seated at the counter with two cups of hot chocolate before her. He had just finished putting his daughter to bed.

"Thanks for taking very good care of her, Mom. She told me she had a nice time with you and Aunt Beth," Tyler said as he positioned himself on the stool opposite her.

Smiling, she slid his beverage across the counter to him and said, "How was your date with Erin?"

"I broke things off with her."

"Oh. I'm sorry about that. She seems like a nice person."

Tyler shrugged. "She is."

Eyeing her son with inquisitive eyes, she said, "Are you okay? You look like you're in pain?"

Sighing, he said, "Mom, she didn't give Lili away."

His mom placed her cup on the counter. "What do you mean?"

Tyler explained to her all that happened with Kaiya the previous day, of course keeping the part about their kiss out of it.

"Mon dieu, to think I treated her like dirt whenever we met. Oh, I'm so sorry she went through all that. What kind of parents would do such a thing? Horrible!" Then she blushed. "Who am I to cast aspersions on their character? I'm not an ideal mother."

Tyler rose from his stool, walked around the counter, and hugged her. "Don't you ever say that again, Mom. You're the world's best mom, and I cherish you. You never intentionally caused me pain. You were only in a bad place which you got out of. For eight years, Kaiya's father lied to her. Even when he saw how depressed she was, he never had compassion enough to tell her the truth. Not even when her mother found out."

She smiled through the tears in her eyes. "Thanks, Tyler. I cherish you, too." Then she let out a sigh. "I feel so sorry for Kaiya. All these years she was left in the dark to mourn a nonexistent dead baby. How cruel."

Tyler nodded. "Indeed."

Suddenly, her face scrunched in a frown, and her eyes held apprehension.

"Kaiya is going to try to take Lili from us."

"What?" Tyler shook his head.

"Now that she knows her daughter is alive; she will want her daughter back. Tyler, you have to do something."

He placed his hands on her shoulders. "Mom, please, calm down. Kaiya isn't going to take Lili away from us. She can't do that. All she wants is to get to know her daughter."

His mom shook her head vigorously. "That's what you think. If I were in Kaiya's shoes, I would want my child with me full time. She might start with wanting to know her, and then before we know it, we're in court fighting for custody of our little girl."

Tyler ran his fingers through his hair. His mom was getting hysterical over nothing. Kaiya would never in a million years do that to him and their daughter. He wouldn't even think of the reasons why he still trusted her. "I assure you that won't be the case, Mom. Please believe me."

His mom placed her hands against her quivering lips. "I'm scared. Why don't we move again?"

Tyler shook his head, debating on how best to get through to the woman for her to know that Kaiya wasn't a threat to them. Poor Kaiya only wanted to be with the daughter she was denied of for eight years.

"Mom, please listen to me. You don't have to be afraid. Kaiya won't take Lili from us. I promise." Then he wrapped her in his arms, praying she would believe him and not give herself unnecessary stress about the whole issue.

"Are you sure?"

"I'm a hundred percent positive that your fears will never come to pass. Kaiya isn't that kind of a person."

"She might have changed. After all, you haven't seen her in eight years."

"Mom, everything will be fine."

"If you say so," his mom stated, but Tyler was definite that she didn't believe him. She would just have to see that Kaiya wouldn't take Lili from them.

Chapter 12

"**A**re you nervous?" Jalissa asked Kaiya over the phone.

"Are you kidding me?" Kaiya's eyes widened as she asked the question. "The inside of my cheeks are in tatters. I've almost chewed them to shreds."

Jalissa's hearty laughter burst through the phone lines. "Oh, Kai, you'll be fine. Just take one step at a time. And you don't have to worry; your little girl is already crazy about you."

Still chewing the insides of her cheeks, Kaiya remarked, "She is crazy about Kaiya her dance teacher. I don't know how she'll feel about me being her mom and abandoning her."

"You didn't abandon her Kai and you can't keep blaming yourself either. It's going to be smooth sailing after you tell her."

"Lissa, what will I do without you?" she questioned, grateful for her friend's pep talk.

"I don't even wanna think about the boring existence you'd have without me," Jalissa laughed with gusto.

Kaiya laughed as well. "I'm coming up to the house now. I'll call you when I get home."

"Alright. Have a pleasant day. Kisses to my niece."

Kaiya ended the call and let out a deep breath. Tyler had called her the previous day to inform her that Lili was back home. Kaiya had wanted to protest coming over so they could tell Lili that she was her mother.

"No, Kaiya. Please don't do that. I'm sure that Lili will love to have you as her mother. She already talks nonstop about you."

Those words had warmed her heart but hadn't stopped the jitters she felt.

"I know, but—"

"No buts. The earlier, the better, Kaiya. I thought that you would be very eager to have her know that you're her mother," Tyler had said in a tone that reflected his surprise.

Biting her lip, she had responded tautly, "I can't wait to tell her, but at the same time, I can't help being scared that she might not fully accept me; that she might insist that Lena is her mother and she doesn't want me to take her place."

Tyler had chuckled. "Is this the brave woman who had stood up to her parents talking?"

Her face had reddened at those words. Yes, she was acting like a coward. The problem stemmed from when she had time to think as she laid on her bed the previous night and couldn't sleep. In the first place, she had been so joyous; she had wished that she could conjure her daughter right there to tell her the truth. But when she recalled all the happy pictures Lili took with her supposed mom, Lena, insecurity had stolen up her mind, causing her to question Lili's acceptance in her life.

"Just come over, Kaiya. Everything will be fine. I promise you," Tyler had said before ending the call.

Well, she was here now, and she prayed within her that everything would indeed be fine. She didn't know what she would do if Lili refused to accept her as her mom.

Feeling self-conscious in her cream-colored silk jumpsuit, which, if truth be told, she had adorned for Tyler's sake, she stepped out from the cab and strode to Tyler's front door. She was more comfortable in sweatshirts and leggings.

Kaiya rang the doorbell and waited. A minute later, the door opened to reveal Tyler looking good in a red chambray shirt and blue jean trousers. His wet black hair was swept back from his forehead. Kaiya itched to run her fingers through the wet mane. She colored slightly.

"Wow, you look amazing." Tyler's appreciative eyes roamed her figure, causing a warm flush to run through her body.

"Not overdressed?" she asked with a nervous smile.

"Certainly not. Except instead of tying your hair in a ponytail, you should let it loose. When it runs wild across your shoulders, it makes you look younger, ravishing."

Kaiya smiled, storing that piece of information for future use.

"Come on in," he invited by opening the door wider.

Keeping herself from chewing her nails which were freshly manicured, Kaiya entered the house, which still took her breath away just like the last time.

"Lili! Kaiya is here!" Tyler called as he led the way to the foyer.

"Lili!" Tyler called again when they waited for a short moment and the little girl didn't show up.

After several minutes passed and Lili didn't surface, Tyler called out to her again. He had to call her name three more times before she responded.

"I'm coming, okay?" Lili replied from somewhere in the house.

The dancer's heart slammed painfully in her chest when she heard footsteps coming down the spiral steps.

"No running down the stairs, young lady," Lili's father shouted when the beautiful little girl came into view.

Casting her dad with a look filled with exasperation, Lili slowed her movements. When she reached Kaiya, she looked past her.

"Aren't you going to say hello to Kaiya?" Tyler asked when the little girl just stood there, staring at Kaiya as if she wasn't there.

"Hello, Kaiya," Lili said with a touch of iciness in her voice that astounded Kaiya. Lili had always been polite to her. She didn't understand why she was acting indifferent all of a sudden.

Before Kaiya got to reply her salutation, Lili turned to her father. "I thought you said Miss Erin was here."

Laughing uneasily, Tyler replied, "No, I didn't. Kaiya is here to spend the whole day with us."

"Yippee," Lili said with an eye roll.

Tyler looked shocked at his daughter's response. His head lifted, and Kaiya read an apology from his eyes. She shrugged and turned to the little girl.

"Hi, Lili. I'm happy to—"

"Could we please go now, Daddy? I'm starving."

Kaiya felt a flush of tears in her eyes which she rapidly beat away. The day wasn't going as planned. She lifted her head to stare at the man whose face had become stiff.

"Alright, Pumpkin. But you must first apologize to Kaiya. It's not only wrong but rude when you cut someone off while they're still talking."

Lowering her head, the little girl said, "I'm sorry, Kaiya."

"It's fine, Lili," Kaiya replied in a small voice.

"Go grab your jacket," Tyler demanded quietly.

Lili hurried to get her jacket from the closet while Kaiya marveled at the beautiful pink dress her daughter had on. She no longer felt she was overdressed.

Tyler had suggested they have a day out before returning to the house to tell Lili the truth about her parentage. Kaiya was all for it. Lili had to be put in the right mood to receive her. The little girl was always cheerful, except today something was off about her.

Tyler took hold of her hand and squeezed it. "I'm sorry about that,"

"It's alright. From what I've seen so far, Tyler, you did a good job raising our little girl," Kaiya confessed with a lot of emotion. He thanked her just as Lili returned.

* * *

Tyler drove them to a nice Italian restaurant in Downtown. Lili ordered pasta. Kaiya wanted mushroom risotto, while Tyler had bacon and lamb lasagna.

"So, Lili, is pasta your favorite meal?" Kaiya asked as a way of striking a conversation with her daughter while they waited for their meal.

"Yes," Lili simply replied without lifting her head from the menu.

"My mom prepared it a lot when she was younger," Tyler explained on his daughter's behalf.

"What about your favorite subject in school?"

"Math."

"You must have inherited that from your dad. When I met him, he was reading through a book of equations." Kaiya looked over at Tyler, and he winked, Kaiya responded with a smile. Lili never raised her head.

"Have you made any friends at school?"

Lili didn't reply because the waiter chose that moment to bring their order. When the man left, she dived into her food, ignoring Kaiya.

After a few more questions in which Lili either answered in monosyllables or kept quiet completely, Kaiya gave up. Tyler answered his daughter's questions when she chose to keep silent.

Through Tyler, she found out that her daughter also liked engaging in arts and crafts just like her. She also discovered other interesting things about the little girl. Kaiya tried to ignore the fact that the little girl seemed to resent her, but she couldn't. Something was wrong. Perhaps she didn't like the fact that they were hanging out outside her dance classes. Kaiya didn't know what to do anymore as all the efforts she made to draw the cheerful little girl out failed. She even went as far as telling her how frightened she was of snakes and anything that crawled, hoping Lili would tell her what frightened her too and they could have a connection from there.

Kaiya was a little bit relieved when the lunch date was over. She couldn't wait to get home to cry out her eyes for the horrible fact that her daughter didn't like her.

"Can we please go to the mall?" Lili begged when they got inside Tyler's car.

"The mall? Why?" Tyler turned in his driver's seat to regard his daughter with questioning eyes.

Shrugging, the little girl replied, "I want to show Kaiya my favorite cat at the pet store."

Kaiya blew her daughter a kiss, happy that she wanted to do something with her.

"I love cats," Kaiya mentioned, but Lili didn't say anything to that.

Reclining back in his seat, Tyler chuckled. "The mall it is then." Then he turned to Kaiya and asked, "I hope you don't mind."

"Of course not."

Tyler gave her a knowing look as if to say he understood why she would jump at the chance of delaying the moment when they would tell Lili the truth.

Blushing, Kaiya looked away.

They arrived at the mall, and Kaiya hoped that her relationship with her daughter would get better.

"Look at that cute dinosaur!" Lili exclaimed when they passed by a game shop with stuffed animals as their prizes on their way to the pet store.

"I'm gonna win it for you, cutie," Kaiya promised as she headed for the stand.

Tyler and Lili followed her to the place. The game was knocking down a statue with some balls. Kaiya looked at it and laughed.

"Piece of cake," she boasted.

Some minutes later, she was, however, scratching her head and wondering what went wrong. No matter how she threw the balls, she always missed the target.

Lili stood beside her giggling while Tyler had his hand across his mouth. Kaiya knew he was laughing at her. Gritting her teeth, she resolved to win the stuffed animal for her daughter at all costs.

"There's no shame if you can't do it, Kaiya," Tyler whispered from the corner of his mouth into her ear.

Giving him a chagrined look, which she made sure Lili didn't see, she turned to focus on the game. From the corner of her eye, she saw Tyler raise his hands with mock surrender.

Concentrating on the game as if her life depended on it, she was finally able to knock down the statue. She threw up her hands with delight.

"Easy peasy," she boasted and then turned to look at Tyler with a glint in her eyes. "In your face," she mouthed at him.

Tyler grinned. Kaiya took the purple dinosaur stuffed animal and wanted to hand it to her daughter, but Lili shook her head and stepped back.

"I don't want it. I never told you to win it for me."

Kaiya felt the tears forming, but she refused to cry. She didn't understand the frostiness from Lili.

Tyler quickly took the stuffed animal from her numbed fingers. "I'm sorry about that."

Kaiya nodded and looked away, trying very hard to control her flailing emotions. It was now clear that her daughter didn't like her. In the next second, Kaiya wondered if she was wrong when Lili took her hand and led her toward the pet store.

Kaiya was looking at very cute cats when Lili dragged her to a stop in front of one of the cages. When Kaiya saw the big snake in the cage, she paled, and a scream tore from her throat. Tyler arrived just in time to take her quivering body into his arms.

"Lili, why would you do such a thing after she told you that she was afraid of snakes?" Tyler chided his daughter.

Kaiya, who was trying to control her anxiety, couldn't see the girl's face to know if she was remorseful. The little girl's words showed she wasn't.

"I'm sorry, I forgot." Then she giggled.

"Kyla Liliana Landry, apologize to Kaiya immediately," Tyler sternly demanded.

Kaiya felt silly when she pulled away from Tyler's arms. She quickly took some steps away from the snake's cage.

"I'm sorry, Kaiya," Lili said stiffly.

"It's okay, sweetie," Kaiya managed to squeeze out of her constricted throat.

"Let's go get some ice-cream," Tyler said, obviously trying to diffuse the tension between mother and daughter.

They took different flavors of ice-cream and toppings, listened to a music rendition, and decided that it was time to head back home. Kaiya was glad that the outing was over. It had been a disaster in her estimation.

As Tyler drove back to the house, she became a mass of nerves all over again. The moment was finally here to tell her daughter that she was her real mother. But she didn't want to anymore.

"Tyler, could we please hold off on telling Lili the truth since she hasn't been in the best of moods all day?"

Tyler shook his head. "Then it's best we tell her to uplift her mood."

Kaiya chewed her bottom lip. "Are you sure?"

"Yes. Everything will be fine. You'll see."

Tyler chose Lili's bedroom as the location for the revelation.

Kaiya marveled again at her daughter's bedroom, which was done in shades of white and pink. Father and mother sat beside their daughter on the bed.

"Lili, we have something very important to tell you," Tyler began softly, pushing back a strand of the little girl's dark hair from her head.

"You two are dating?" Lili asked with a frown on her face.

Tyler rapidly shook his head. "No, sweetie, what I want to tell you may come as a shock to you, but I want you to know it's the truth, and we all love you very much."

"What is it, Daddy?"

"I told you already that Kaiya was an old friend of mine. What I didn't tell you is that the two of us dated when we were teenagers. She was my girlfriend. What I didn't tell you is that she is your mother."

"Oh." The little girl looked disappointed.

Kaiya, seeing the obvious disappointment on the girl's face, wished she could run out of the room and never return to the house, but she wasn't ready to give up on her daughter after only just finding her. Lili didn't want her as her mother, and she couldn't force the girl to accept her, but she needed to know why her attitude towards her changed. She had thought that the little girl would be joyous since they got along so well at her dance school.

"Lili," Tyler gently called, looking at his daughter with surprise in his eyes. "Is that all you're going to say?"

Lili shrugged, staring at her Cinderella-themed bedcovers. "What do you want me to say, Daddy? I don't want Kaiya as my mommy. My mommy is in heaven."

Kaiya drew in a ragged breath and was about rising from the bed, but Tyler stopped her with a hand on her arm.

His eyes begged her to stay. "Please don't go. I'll get to the bottom of this."

Kaiya forced color back to her pasty face even as Lili stared at her rudely.

"Lili," Tyler began again.

Folding her hands across her chest, Lili shouted. "She is not my mommy.

109

My mommy is in heaven!"

Kaiya's heart broke with every harsh word that her daughter spoke. If it wasn't for Tyler's presence in the room, she was as sure as night followed day that she would have rushed out of the room.

"Lili." Tyler's voice was gentle but at the same time, firm. "What's going on?"

Still with her head bowed, Lili replied, "Nothing."

"Pumpkin, you know you can tell me if anything is troubling you, right?"

Lili nodded.

"Then please tell me what's going on. You've not been yourself all day. What's wrong? You're not only hurting her but me as well."

Kaiya's heart broke some more when her daughter raised a tear-stained face to look at her father. She itched to draw her daughter into her arms and comfort her.

Tyler dropped Kaiya's hand to put an arm around his daughter. "Sweetie, please talk to me."

Sniffing, Lili said, "Grandma told Aunt Beth that Kaiya is my mommy. I was happy when she mentioned that Kaiya was my real mommy, but then she said that Miss Kaiya would take me away from you."

At that point, tears poured down Kaiya's face. She felt bad that her daughter had been tormented by such thoughts.

Tyler cuddled his weeping daughter in his arms. "Pumpkin, nobody will take you away from me. All Kaiya wants is to get to know you. She doesn't want to take you away from me."

"Sweetie, I promise that I have no intention of taking you away from your daddy. Why, he has done such a good job raising you. The thought never crossed my mind. All I want is to get to know you if that's okay with you?"

Raising her head from her father's arms, she nodded and sniffed. "I'm sorry I was rude to you all day. I thought that if I was that way to you, you wouldn't want to take me away."

Kaiya, understanding why her daughter had been bratty all day, nodded. "I understand, Lili. I promise I'll never take you away from your dad or your grandma."

"Daddy, I thought Mommy in heaven is my real mom."

Kaiya decided to cut in. She held her daughter's hand. "Lili, your mommy in heaven is always going to be your mom." It took everything in Kaiya to say that. She should have been with her little girl from the day she was born. "But I'm also your mom because you came out of my tummy." She took her daughter's hand and placed it against her stomach.

Carefully removing her hand from her mom's, Lili Said, "I don't understand. If you're my real mommy, where were you?"

Fighting back tears that were threatening to overwhelm her, Kaiya replied, "I didn't leave you, Sweetie. I could never leave you. I only just found out about you. I've thought about you every day that you weren't with me."

Her daughter still looked confused and she couldn't blame her. Kaiya's heart broke. The situation was bizarre, Kaiya resolved herself to her feelings of never forgiving her father for doing this to her and her baby. She didn't know how to explain the situation in a way her daughter would understand.

"Lili," Tyler held his daughter's other hand. "What Kaiya is saying is true. I know it is confusing to you. After you came out of Kaiya's tummy, the doctors and Kaiya's dad told her that you had gone to heaven."

"But I didn't go to heaven, I'm right here."

"I know Sweetie. People made me believe that you went to heaven even though you were given to your daddy as soon as you came out of my tummy. I didn't know that you didn't go to heaven until I met your daddy again and I learned the truth.

That's why we're telling you now, so you know the truth."

Still looking a bit befuddled, Lili said, "But why did they tell you I died."

Unable to hold back the tears further for what her father did to her, she said, "They thought they were protecting me." Kaiya couldn't believe that she was trying to make her parents seem less wicked than they are. Lili was her little girl and she didn't want her daughter to feel any hatred for anyone. Even though they deserved it. "They thought that because I was so young, that I wouldn't be able to take care of you. But they were wrong, and you want to know why? Her daughter nodded. "Because even before you came out of my tummy, I already loved you so much because you were and still are the best part of me and the best part of your dad. I'm so glad you were given to your dad."

After digesting that for a moment, Lili asked, "You're really my mom?"

Kaiya nodded and smiled through her tears. "Yes, I am."

"Will the people take me away again?"

"Your dad and I will never let anyone take you from us, okay?"

"Nobody is taking you away from me, Pumpkin."

Their daughter nodded and seemed satisfied.

Lili left her father's arms to give her mother a tight hug. Tears continued to pour down Kaiya's face as she ensconced her daughter in a bear hug. Tyler looked on with a smile on his face.

When they both put their emotions in control and wiped away their tears, Kaiya explained to her daughter as gently as possible the reason she hadn't been in her life. Lili had many questions, and Kaiya answered them as honestly as she could.

Tyler cut in softly, "Pumpkin, if it's okay with you, Kaiya would love to spend some time with you."

Kaiya lifted her head with surprise. She loved the idea even though they hadn't discussed it prior. Just then, Tyler lifted his head and gave her a questioning gaze as if asking if his suggestion was okay.

Kaiya nodded and gave him a bright smile of gratitude.

Lili shrugged. "Okay." Then she focused her gaze on her mother and said, "I'm allergic to nuts."

"Got that." Kaiya made gestures with her hand as if opening her brain and throwing the piece of information in it.

Lili giggled.

Tyler continued talking to his daughter into getting used to Kaiya being around in their lives from now on. Kaiya watched them with love in her eyes. She loved how gentle he was with their little girl and suddenly longed to be a part of their lives permanently and forever.

After having a tea party with Lili, it was time for Kaiya to go home. She was sorry that such a beautiful day was coming to an end, but there wasn't much she could do about it. It made her yearn for them to be a family.

* * *

When they dropped her off at home, Kaiya invited them in. Lili was more than eager to see her home, which she thought was super cool. Kaiya was just thankful that her daughter didn't hate her anymore.

"You've got cats," the little girl crooned when she set her eyes on Sir and Lady. Then she bestowed her dad with a knowing look. "See? There's no harm in having cats, Daddy."

Tyler chuckled. "Only if you can take care of them."

Lili gave him a face, which made both parents laugh. Lili joyfully played with the cats that enjoyed being stroked, and then Kaiya put on some music and moved her body to the rhythm. Tyler and Lili later joined her, and they all had a fun time dancing.

The beautiful day concluded with a *Cinderella* Disney movie that they all watched cuddled together on Kaiya's super soft new couch.

"Oh, she's asleep," Kaiya noticed when the movie credits rolled in.

"She had a super fun day," Tyler commented, cradling his daughter in his arms.

Kaiya bit her bottom lip. "I know this is super sudden, but why don't you both spend the night? I have a spare bed and this couch. I don't think it would be fair rousing her and taking her home. It's quite late."

After a moment's hesitation, Tyler agreed with a small shrug. Happily, Kaiya left to prepare her old room for her daughter. Tyler carried the little girl into the room, and Kaiya tucked her in.

They came back into the living room and settled on the couch. Kaiya fiddled with the remote control.

"Do you want to watch a movie?" Kaiya asked when the tensed silence had gone on long enough between them.

"No, I have something better in mind," Tyler said hoarsely and dragged her into his arms. He made her straddle him and captured her lips with his.

"Gosh, I've been longing to do that all day," he confessed, smiling and reaching for her zip. "When that lady painted a frog on my face, all I could think of was getting you to kiss me so that I could become your prince charming."

Kaiya laughed. She wanted nothing more than to cap the day off with great sex, but she was worried. She stopped Tyler's hands. His brows hit his forehead.

"I'm not going to have sex with another woman's man," she forcefully told him.

His forehead scrunched into a frown. "What are you talking about?"

Folding her arms across her chest and giving him a stern look, she said, "I'm talking about Erin."

Grinning, he replied, "There's absolutely nothing going on between Erin and me, I promise."

"But—"

The words died in her throat when Tyler cradled her head and placed his lips on hers. The kiss went on and on before something penetrated Kaiya's brain. She wrenched her lips from his.

"We have to stop."

Tyler scowled. "Are you going to talk me to death instead of allowing me the pleasure of your delectable body?"

His words sent a warm glow marking her face, but she held back when he tried to kiss her again.

"I'm not on the pill," she blurted out and reddened. "Last time...I...um...I mean in the washroom, we didn't use any protection, and fortunately, we escaped another unplanned pregnancy." Her period came a week after their tryst, and she didn't know how she felt about that, and she wouldn't dwell on it. "I don't—"

"Fortunately, all I've been thinking of is making love to you again and again, so I have packs of condoms in my wallet."

She let out a sigh of relief.

"Now, any other business because I'm about to rip a hole in my jeans!"

Kaiya giggled as she felt his rising manhood. For an answer, she lowered her head and kissed him.

Tyler carried her up to her room and made slow and passionate love to her that left her eyes watering at the sweetness of it. They spent the whole night pleasuring each other but rose early the following morning to avoid questions from their smart daughter.

Chapter 13

Kaiya checked her reflection on the mirror again just to make sure she was looking good for her daughter and her- Tyler. It was two days since they told Lili the truth about her parentage. Tyler had called the previous day to ask her if she would be free to go out with them the following day. Kaiya had laughingly told him that even if she wasn't, she would clear her schedule for them, which she had done.

Now dressed in a shift dress, Kaiya wondered once again if she wasn't overdressed for the occasion. Possibly, Tyler just wanted a casual hangout, and she felt as if she was dressed for a movie premiere.

Kaiya giggled. She was feeling this way because she was usually in sweat-shirts and leggings. With Tyler back in her life, and with the knowledge that he loved her in dresses, she clothed herself that way to please him. Her curls were let loose across her shoulders.

She shook her head. What pleasing a man would make a woman do! However, she had to admit that she loved her new look.

The sound of the doorbell made jittery. With one last glance at her reflection, she turned away and rushed to the living room to get the door. Lili instantly threw her arms around her, which sent warmth rolling through her body. Tyler's appreciative gaze raked her body.

"Are you ready?" he asked with a sensual voice, and she wondered for a moment if he was actually referring to the outing or something else.

Blushing because of her errant thoughts, she nodded and picked her purse. Hand in hand with her daughter, they walked to Tyler's car and got in.

"We'll go out for lunch, but I want to show you the site where I work," he explained quietly.

A warm smile crossed Kaiya's face.

"I hope you don't mind," he said when she remained silent.

She smiled at him. "I don't mind at all. In fact, I can't wait to see you in action."

Tyler laughed heartily. He drove at a sedate pace to the mall; the building was still ongoing.

"Wow! It's huge!" Kaiya exclaimed at the site of the building when Tyler drove to the parking lot.

Tyler grinned. "It's going to house a lot of businesses."

"Perhaps I should set up one of my dancing schools here," she teased as she released her seatbelt.

Tyler laughed again. "I'll get you a slot."

Kaiya giggled and helped her daughter out of the car. Tyler reached for his construction helmet at the backseat and put it on. She also noticed that he had on his special work boots. Just the sight of him in his work gear turned her on. He looked every inch an architect holding site plans.

Kaiya noticed that immediately they stepped into the building, several men also wearing similar helmets to Tyler quickly walked up to them and shook hands with him. The whole place was quite noisy with several equipment in use. Tyler introduced her and Lili to the site foreman.

"Wait. Did you design this?" Kaiya asked after gawking at the place with wondrous eyes. Tyler had told her earlier that it would have ten floors. The building itself had the shape of a pentagon.

He nodded. "Let me show you girls around."

With her daughter's hand in hers, Kaiya allowed Tyler lead the way around the uncompleted building. When they got upstairs, Kaiya saw Finn at a distance and waved at him. He nodded at them with a bright smile across his face and crossed the plane to reach them.

"Hi, Kaiya," Finn said when he got to them and hugged her. He squatted and hugged Lili, too. "Hi, Lili."

Lili smiled shyly at him. "Hi, Finn."

Finn shook hands with Tyler before turning towards Kaiya and saying,

"Came to see Tyler in action?"

Kaiya blushed and smiled. "It's spectacular."

Finn nodded. "It is, isn't it?"

Tyler led them away after a brief discussion with Finn. Kaiya had her eyes engorged the whole time Tyler took her around the place. He showed her where various luxury stores would be situated, valet parking, fountains and gardens, helipad, place for a live band, a cinema, a casino, showrooms, auto saloons, and so on.

Kaiya saw another side to Tyler which she greatly admired. She saw how different he was with his employees. Although he was quite demanding, he was also fair. She enjoyed listening to him interact with his employees. He asked about the health of one of his employee's wife who was at the hospital, as well as another employee who was ill.

As he took her and Lili around the place, Kaiya had to admit that Tyler was indeed a very good architect. She couldn't wait to see the building when it was completed. They said their goodbyes to Finn and walked to the car.

"Thanks for bringing me here, Ty. It was wonderful. You do know your onions," Kaiya commented when she settled herself on the car seat beside him.

"Dad, I want to be the first person to visit the place when it's completed," Lili cut in from the back seat.

Her parents laughed.

"Sure, Pumpkin. Anything you want," Tyler promised, winking at her from the rear-view mirror.

He drove them to a nice restaurant around the corner where they all had a wonderful time.

* * *

Later on that week, Kaiya was surprised when Tyler asked her to accompany him to Lili's school for a parent-teacher conference. She was glad that he thought to include her, when he didn't have to. It was one thing to have their family and the people closest to them know that she was Lili's mom, but she can't help but feel this meeting would make it official.

She cleared her schedule and asked on of her on call teachers to cover her afternoon classes. She stood at the entrance of Lili's school and nervously rubbed her hands together. For a moment she wondered if she needed to change, regretting the fact that almost her entire wardrobe seemed to consist of sweatshirts and leggings, but she threw the idea away. This meeting was about Lili and not about how her new found mother wore.

Remembering what Tyler had said about her hair, she removed the band from her hair, letting it flow down her neck. Not a moment too soon, he pulled up into the parking lot and she got into the car and shot him a playful look.

"You're late," she grinned at him.

He grinned back, "Traffic babe," and went back to navigating the road while her heart skipped a few hundred beats.

He called her babe!

She wondered if the dynamics of their relationship had changed. Sex was one thing and amazing as it was, she was finding it hard to get into the flow of a romantic relationship.

It was more complicated than her most complicated dance move and that was saying a lot. They had Lili to consider this time around.

She kept quiet throughout the ride, lost in her thoughts and Tyler didn't press her, only tapping her hand lightly when they were in the school's parking lot.

The parking lot was filled with cars, with parents coming out of their cars and getting into the school. Tyler got out of the car and quickly rushed to open her door. She thanked him as she got out. He took hold of her hand, leading her into the school. They followed the throng of bodies in the hallway and then into a space that was not as big as an auditorium but larger than a classroom.

They found seats somewhere in the middle of the room and sat. As soon as they sat, Tyler took her hand again and distracted her throughout the conference with his finger running circles in her palm. She barely heard a word the headteacher was saying as every nerve in her body was tingling from his touch.

All too soon it was over and they stood, leaving for individual meetings with their children's class teachers. Kaiya fought to control her excitement. She was a parent now and privy to parent teacher meetings. She looked up at Tyler's smiling face and was thankful to him for including her in their daughter's educational journey.

Lili's teacher was a petite Asian woman who was all smiles as she told them of Lili's extraordinary school performance.

"She's very smart and very perceptive," the woman who had introduced herself as Mrs. Harris. Mr's Harris looked outside through the classroom window and looked lovingly at Lili who played with the other kids on the playground. Kaiya's heart swelled with pride when she heard that. She continued to listen to the woman who had a sweet tone in her voice when talking about their daughter.

"And she's just so kind to her peers, however she allows no one to push her around. When she grasps something new that I teach and her classmates don't understand, she tries very hard to explain the concept to them to them." Mrs. Harris had nothing but praises for Lili, and Kaiya felt like a proud mom even though she had nothing to do with Lili's upbringing.

Before they left, Tyler turned to Mrs. Harris, "I'd like you to put Lili's mother down as an emergency contact." Kaiya's heart expanded but he wasn't done, "And on occasion, she might pick Lili up from school."

Mrs. Harris looked like she wanted to say something, but she smiled and wrote down Kaiya's information in a medium sized book on the side of her desk. They went to the room that overlooked the playground and watched Lili with the other kids.

"Thanks for making me an emergency contact for our daughter. It means a lot to me."

"You don't have to thank me. We never had any official custody papers drawn up. Legally, she is ours equally. I spoke to my lawyer earlier."

"Lawyer, why?"

Did he want to create a formal custody agreement?

"You look nervous. You don't have to be. I called to inquire about our situation and see if I could get your rights as Lili's mom reinstated but the lawyer told me that legally, we both have equal rights. The document your dad gave me with your signature that stipulates you signed your parental rights away isn't legal since a judge never approved it. It's as if we were a couple with a child and then one day you left, leaving your child behind without any legal document saying you've given up custody." He must have read the horror on her face because he quickly added, "The lawyer's words not mine."

"You wanted to get my parental rights reinstated?" He was so sweet to think of doing that for her. She hadn't even thought of the legal implications. Her only concern was spending time with her daughter and getting to know her better.

"You never agreed to give up our child. I want us to parent our amazing kid together."

"Thanks Ty, this means everything to me. I hope I don't let Lili down." *You either.*

"Kai, you're an amazing mom already. Don't be too hard on yourself, okay?"

"Okay." She gave him a small smile.

They discussed mundane things while they waited for Lili to be done with her lessons. "You know," Kaiya began, "She got her smarts from you. I still remember the boy who hid in a toilet at a party to study." She nudged him and they laughed.

"Well she got her beauty and her spunk from you. That stubbornness couldn't have come from anywhere else." Tyler smiled, a fond expression taking over his face. She smiled, her eyes catching his as he leaned in. She leaned in too, almost unconsciously, their lips met.

The kiss was soft, an expression of all the things they felt but were afraid to say.

"Daddy!"

The shout made them jump apart then laugh like teenagers as Lili barreled towards them. She jumped into her father's outstretched arms first, then into her mother's.

"Well sweetie, how was school?"

"Good. I thought Grandma was going to pick me up." Her brows furrowed in confusion and Tyler laughed. "We thought it'd be a great idea to stay behind after your parent teacher conference."

Lili grinned, her entire row of teeth showing, "Let's go home!"

"Speaking of home," Tyler gave Kaiya a sly look, "how do you feel about spending the weekend at your mom's?"

Kaiya gasped, amazed for the second time that day of his willingness to include her in all things Lili. Lili squealed in delight.

Kaiya was already making a mental list of things she would need to get for that spare bedroom in her condo. She wished she had known Tyler's plans in advance, nonetheless she was happy.

Lili was chattering happily to both her parents as they entered the car and began the drive home, "I need my pajamas, my toothbrush because Mrs. Harris said we should brush twice a day," she said to her parents like she was passing sagely advice. They chuckled.

"You need to floss once a day," Kaiya added.

"I hate flossing," Lili said and continued to list the things she needed until they got to Tyler's house. Lili zipped out of the car and run towards the house. Tyler's mother let Lili in after she rang the doorbell.

Kaiya faced Tyler as soon as her little girl was inside of the house. "Tyler, I can't believe you'd do this so soon."

He turned towards her with a confused expression on his face, "I thought you'd be happy to spend more one on one time with her."

"I am. I'm just surprised you'd suggest it so soon."

He smiled softly and brought his body as close to hers as he could in the car and took her hands in his.

"Lili is your daughter and she loves you. You two will be fine."

Kaiya groaned, "You always could see right through me. I just feel like something's going to go horribly wrong and she'd hate me forever."

"Did I ever tell you about that time that I fed our three-week-old daughter regular milk instead of formula or that she thought peeing standing up was the normal thing to do for almost a month before my mom broke the habit and taught her that girls peed sitting down?"

"You fed our three-week-old regular milk?" She was surprised by that admission. Even her sixteen-year-old self knew babies didn't drink regular milk.

Tyler shook his head and kissed Kaiya on her forehead. "My point is every parent make mistakes, but great parents learn from their mistakes."

Lili bounded out the front door with a small pink gym bag, "I'm ready!"

"Are we there yet?" Lili asked as soon as she was settled in the backseat. Tyler and Kaiya shared an amused look, "No sweetie we're not."

She groaned and kept quiet for a whole of five minutes before piping up again, "Are we there yet?"

Kaiya smiled at her, "Lili darling, you've been to my home, you'll know when we get there." Lili nodded, placated.

The car finally pulled up next to her condo building and Lili was out of the car before it fully lurched to a stop. "Lili! Be careful." Kaiya felt her heart fly to her throat before settling back into her chest.

Lili stood the building's front door, giggling and tapping her feet in an impatient manner. Kaiya got out of the car and asked her daughter to return to the car to tell her father goodbye. Lili obeyed and shuffled back to the car.

Kaiya saw as Tyler got out of the car and reprimanded Lili for running out of a moving car. After Tyler was satisfied with Lili's responses, he lifted Lili off the ground in a hug and placed kisses all over her face. Lili shrieked with glee. Tyler set Lili on her feet.

Tyler looked back at Kaiya and smiled and she waved as Lili rushed back to where Kaiya stood. Tyler got back into his car and called out to Lili, "I love you Pumpkin. Listen to your mom."

He drove off looking very happy. For a moment she wondered if he was heading out on a date. Her heart constricted at the thought and she had to breathe through her paranoia.

She looked down at her daughter, feeling a bit awkward. She had been alone with Lili plenty of times, but this was the first time they were alone since she had found out she was Lili's mother.

She took hold of her child's small hand and opened the door over her head. Lili rushed in and they headed towards the elevators. In the elevators, Kaiya instructed Lili on what number to press. When they finally entered her condo unit, Lili heading straight for the cats lounging around the house. She grabbed Lady and cuddled her so hard that Lady yowled.

Kaiya laughed and told Lili to be gentler. Kaiya went about making dinner – kraft dinner for herself and Lili. She kept Lili busy by allowing her to fill the cat bowls with food and water. Her daughter seemed to enjoy the task even though she made a mess.

Kaiya learned more about her daughter as they sat and ate their steaming plates of food. Kaiya subscribed to Disney plus and mother and daughter watched The Parent Trap.

Bedtime came too soon, and she tucked Lili into the bed in the spare bedroom and read the little mermaid to her. Halfway through, Lili fell asleep, a serene smile on her face.

Kaiya smiled at her and whispered softly, "And they lived happily ever after." She kissed Lili on her forehead and tiptoed out of the room, closing the door softly. She rested her head on the door and sighed.

She thought it was surreal, two months ago, she was grieving the loss of her son, and in a way the loss of her heart. Now she had a beautiful baby girl.

The next day came early, the sun streaming through her windows and waking her up. She padded to Lili's room – the guest bedroom, but in her head she had started calling it Lili's room. She would redecorate the room so Lili would be more comfortable any time she came over.

The little girl was awake and full of boundless energy, already asking what her plans were for the day.

"Well," she spared a smile for the grinning girl as she whisked eggs, "I was thinking of going shopping and wanted to invite Milania and your Aunt Kalilah. What do you think?"

Lili squealed, running over to hug her mother, "Yes! Yes! Yes!" Kaiya laughed, deriving joy from her daughter's happiness.

Two hours later Kalilah came by to pick them up with her driver. Kaiya opened the back door of Kalilah's car so that she and Lili could climb into the car. Both Milania and Lili squealed when they saw each other and proceeded to have disjointed conversations that Kaiya and Kalilah found hard to keep up with no matter how hard she tried to listen in.

"You're glowing sis... You aren't pregnant, are you?" Kalilah whispered to her sister after Kaiya was seated.

"Of course not, I'm just happy to be spending time with my daughter!"

"Hmm." That was the extent of Kalilah's response.

"Where are my nephews?"

"They're with the nanny. I really needed this break." Kaiya squeezed her sister's hand knowing how much of a handful the kids were.

They arrived at Angrignon mall and both little girls were enthusiastic. The quartet went from store to store. Unashamed to admit it, Kaiya bought everything Lili wanted. She had so much to make up for and getting Lili's heart's desire was a small dent in the debt she owed her daughter.

The group ate a small lunch and Kaiya learned from Kalilah that their mother was still broken hearted over what happened. Kaiya couldn't bring herself to feel sorry for her mother. Her mother should have told her the truth. After that thought, Lili asked that they go to Claire's next and Kaiya obliged her daughter.

"Kaiya, we can keep all the clothes you bought me at your house. When I come over for a sleepover, I won't have to pack anything." Kaiya kissed her daughter's forehead as she paid for the last of their purchases at Claire's.

"Let's go do our nails," Kalilah said.

"Good idea and maybe we can have ice cream after." Kaiya responded and hustled both little girls towards the nail salon. They all chose their colors. Kaiya and Lili picked the same pink color. Kalilah got a gel set done and it looked very nice. Kaiya chose shellac.

"Your nails are pretty Aunty Kalilah," Lili said in wonderment. Kaiya felt envious of her daughter referring to her sister as her aunt Kalilah but still called her by her name.

When their nails were dried, Kaiya sent selfies and pictures of their nails to Tyler.

Tyler's reply was full of heart emojis which made her smile as she tapped the characters on her phone. She smiled at his response.

"Who wants ice cream?" Kalilah asked.

"Me! Me!" Her niece and daughter squealed.

"Let's go then."

* * *

"Where are we going, Ty?" Kaiya asked for the umpteenth time.

Tyler sighed beside her in his car. "You were always very inquisitive. I thought you would have outgrown it by now."

Kaiya giggled. "Look who is talking. Take away my blindfold, and then I'll stop asking."

Tyler chuckled. "No, I'm not going to do that. You look as sexy as I want in it, so you better get used to it until we get to our destination."

Kaiya let out a deep breath. "At least give me a clue."

Clicking his tongue in mock exasperation, he replied, "It's somewhere between Longueuil and Montreal Island, and that's all you're going to get from me, and you better not start guessing or I'll turn the car around this minute."

"Someone is mighty testy this morning," she remarked, laughing. "You pick me up from work, blindfold me and go on a long drive, yet you don't expect me to be inquisitive about it?"

"Put like that, I don't blame you for being curious. Just trust me, okay? It's a surprise you're going to love. I assure you that you won't regret the outing."

Kaiya shrugged with a look of resignation on her face. "Okay. If you say so."

Tyler chuckled. "I do say so. Now shut that sexy mouth of yours, and let's enjoy some music."

Tyler slot in his favorite Maroon 5 CD and they both sang along until they reached their destination.

"I want you to promise me that you won't scream when I remove your blindfold because I'm afraid my eardrums might never remain the same again when you see what I have planned for us," Tyler teased as he reached for the black band around her eyes.

126

"Sir, you ask for too much," Kaiya returned and laughed. "Adrenaline is already pumping through my veins as I'm hearing screams. I think I know where we are."

Tyler shook his head. "Woman, you have no idea."

Carefully, Tyler removed the blindfold, and just as he guessed, Kaiya screamed into his ear.

"La Ronde!" she exclaimed with so much excitement that he grinned broadly. It was the one place they never visited in their youth as a couple. He saw it as a perfect opportunity to do so now. Lili was in school, and his mom would pick her up later.

Kaiya turned to Tyler with tears in her eyes. "This brings back so many memories. I remember all the times we planned to come here, and for one reason or another, we were never able to make it."

Tyler agreed with her with a nod and a smile. "Now is a good a time as any."

She shocked him by leaning closer and placing a sensual kiss on his lips. She pulled away and wiped her red lipstick off his lips.

"After that kiss, I'm tempted to start the car and find the nearest hotel around here," he hoarsely told her, his eyes promising all sorts of sensual delight.

Her joyous laughter rang out in the car, making Tyler glad that he had planned this outing with her.

"We should have brought Lili along," Kaiya mentioned as she let herself out of the car.

Tyler shook his head. "Nope. This one is for us. We can bring her with us another day."

As they reached the gate, Kaiya said happily. "I'm going on every ride the place has to offer."

Tyler blew out an exasperated breath. "It's going to be a long day."

Kaiya laughed as he paid their tickets, and they entered the very large amusement park that was thriving with people who were having so much fun.

"So, where do we begin?" He put an arm around Kaiya's shoulder.

"You know where," she answered by giving him a knowing look.

"Indeed, I do," he replied and chuckled.

They had always wanted to ride the famous Le Monstre rollercoaster.

"Le Monstre it is."

"And then, Goliath."

Tyler laughed and led the way to where the gigantic rollercoaster was situated. Kaiya screamed all through the ride while Tyler watched her, laughing and enjoying the way she was having so much fun.

From the Le Monstre, they rode the Goliath and other rollercoasters in the place. By the time they were done, Tyler wasn't up for anything high again. But Kaiya would hear nothing of it.

"I can't believe you're giving up already. Did you see that couple we came in with? Well, they're already one ride ahead of us."

Tyler could only laugh when Kaiya took his hand and led him to a small waterslide. He was seeing firsthand how competitive Kaiya was, and he loved it. The waterslide was so much fun that Tyler couldn't help yearning to do it again.

"See? I told you it was going to be fun," Kaiya said as she led him up the ride again. With his arms around her, they both went down the slide, screaming with excitement.

"I feel like a teenager all over again," Kaiya commented as they headed to the next slide.

Tyler laughed. He was pleased that he had brought Kaiya here. She seemed to be living her teenage fantasy. He loved watching how her eyes sparkled whenever she was to face a new challenge in the park and the way her lips would curve in a smile whenever she was done with a ride. This day would forever remain fresh and treasured in his heart.

They watched a show, dined at a restaurant before walking hand in hand around the place. When it was time for them to leave as it became dark, Kaiya was sorry to go but happy that she came.

"Thank you, Tyler, for such a wonderful day," she remarked in a tired voice after he helped her into the car.

Tyler reached for her and placed his lips on hers in a passionate kiss. "I should be the one thanking you for such a swell time, Kai. You really made my day with the way you enjoyed every ride and thrill here."

Kaiya threw her arms around him and kissed him warmly. "Thanks for that."

"You're very welcome. I need to tell you something as well." He said somberly and saw a look of panic on her face and continued quickly before she got the wrong idea. "I'm happy that you've reunited with our daughter and spending time getting to know her. You and me, we've been getting along great and I want it to continue. I want us to take full advantage of this second chance we've been given. I want you to know that I am very much interested in finding out what's in store for us and our future. I wanna see where this thing goes with you. I need to know that you feel the same."

"Are you sure Ty? I love spending time with you, and I am very much interested in finding out where this will all lead, however we still have some things to work out."

"I know," he said then claimed her lips in a kiss.

Tyler had to nudge Kaiya awake when they reached his house. He gently carried her from the car into the house. Thankfully, Lili and his mom had already gone to bed by the time he climbed up the stairs to his room with the sleeping Kaiya in his arms.

Emotion clogged his throat as he watched her sleep. It was as if they had never parted, and he was glad that they had a second chance to find each other again.

Chapter 14

"Kai, will you stop worrying?" Kalilah said to her sister who was busy going through all the goodies put out for the children in the yard.

Kaiya smiled sheepishly at her sister. "You can't blame me, Lah. I'm just being a mother. I don't want anything to happen to Lili. She's allergic to nuts."

Her sister rolled her eyes. "You've told me that like a hundred times already. I told the caterer not to include any nuts in whatever she's bringing over."

Kaiya chewed the inside of her cheek. "I know that, but one can never be too careful."

Kalilah sighed. "If you don't have anything to do, why don't you go and check up on the kids and make sure they're behaving themselves with the clowns I invited?"

Kaiya giggled. "What are you afraid of, Lah? That your kids have taken after me by kicking every clown they see?"

Her sister laughed with gusto. A big smile was plastered across Kaiya's face as she walked away. It wasn't that she hated clowns, but for some reason when they were kids, clowns freaked her out.

Kaiya strode across the yard that was beautifully decorated for the twins' birthday party. There were various attractions for the kids. There were balloons to be popped, a piñata for later, several games and jumping castles, to name a few. Kalilah and Finn had gone out of their way to make their children's birthday spectacular.

Kaiya's eyes fell on Lili who was doing the hoopla hoop with some of the kids. Kaiya had braided her daughter's hair before the party. It was still like a dream to her that she now had a daughter she could do such with. Lili had also tried to braid her mom's hair but hadn't gotten the hang of it yet. She now had her little best friend to shop with and wear matching outfits with. Kaiya felt blessed.

Her daughter's braids flew in the air as she swung around, laughing energetically. A fond smile was splashed across Kaiya's face as she watched Max and Millie, who were dressed in baby blue, run toward their cousin and embrace her. Lili left the hoola hoop and tickled both of them, causing them to laugh heartily.

She reached where the clowns were entertaining the children with various balloon structures and laughed. At least, the children were held in rapt attention, and none of them looked like they were going to either kick or jump on the clowns anytime soon.

Kaiya crossed the yard again to inform her sister that everything was okay with the clowns, and she believed it would continue to stay that way. Her heart soared with joy as she heard the gay laughter of children all around her as they engaged in one fun activity or the other. Their parents were seated at a corner of the yard, also enjoying themselves with barbecue which Finn was handling.

Unable to stop herself, Kaiya went to the table where treats were kept and made sure one more time that there were no nuts in any of them. She caught Kalilah's knowing look across the yard, and laughter fell from her throat. Her sister was bound to think she was paranoid. She didn't care.

Kaiya returned to her sister and said with a twinkle in her eyes, "I'm pleased to inform you that the kids are behaving themselves."

Kaiya turned in the direction of her child and saw Jalissa at a distance inflating balloons for some kids. The wistful look on her face made Kaiya wonder for the umpteenth time why Jalissa continually denied ever wanting children. Whenever her best friend was around kids, there was always this look in her eyes that showed how much yearned for one of her own.

"I'll be right back," she informed her sister briskly and walked to where her friend just finished helping the last child with a balloon.

"Thanks, Missy," the boy said with obvious joy on his face.

Ruffling his brown hair, Jalissa replied with a broad smile of her own,

"You're welcome, sport."

"You know," Kaiya began as she stood beside her friend at the balloon stand, "you can always join the mommy club."

Jalissa's face instantly became pale like every other time Kaiya mentioned babies to her.

"What are you talking about?" Jalissa prevaricated, picking up a balloon.

Kaiya folded her arms across her chest and regarded her friend squarely. "You'd make such a good mom."

Avoiding her gaze, her best friend replied, "I don't know what you're talking about."

Kaiya wondered why the topic of children always got her friend upset.

She placed a comforting hand on her friend's shoulder. "What is it about having kids that always gets you upset, Lis?"

With her face becoming pale, Jalissa turned away. "Please stop seeing something that isn't there, Kai. Your sister assigned me to check on the gifts for the kids. I'll be right back."

Kaiya watched ruefully as her friend walked hurriedly away from her. Kaiya was tempted to go after her, but from times past, she knew it wouldn't get her anywhere. Her friend would only end up avoiding her like a plague which she didn't like.

Perhaps when Jalissa was good and ready, she would talk. Kaiya made up her mind not to pressure her friend into saying why she got all emotional whenever they talked about children. It wasn't fair on her friend. After all, Jalissa hadn't pressured her into talking about the death of her supposed son. She just stood there beside her, offering her shoulder for her to lean on.

On her way back to where her sister was standing by a table filled with snacks for the children, Kaiya's gaze moved to where the adults were hanging out, and her steps faltered. Her heart squeezed in her chest as she watched Tyler carefully carry her baby nephew. She swallowed thickly, but the lump refused to leave. Her eyes watered as she watched him cuddle the baby and smile at him.

This was most likely the way he had carried and cradled Lili when she was a baby, thinking she abandoned them. She never got to cradle her daughter.

Never felt the infant against her chest, nursing at her breasts. Her father had taken that away from her.

Quickly, Kaiya sniffed back the tears threatening to spill down her face. This was a joyous occasion, and there was no place for tears, even though her heart was wrenching in pain at what she had lost. Although she had the love of her daughter, it still hurt that she had missed so much in her daughter's.

For many years, she had thought she would never have another child; dedicated to giving her love to her son and afraid that she might lose another child just the way she lost the first one. However, now that she saw the wonderful sight of Tyler handling a baby, she ached for another child; a child that she would be able to be part of his or her life from the beginning. Unconsciously, her hand went to her flat stomach. Her mind ran wild, imagining Tyler's second child nestled there. How wonderful the experience would be this time, unlike last time when she had been so afraid and filled with anxiety.

"Kaiya, quit drooling over that man and come over here. I've got something to tell you."

"You know, Lah," Kaiya said when she reached her grinning sister, "you have the discreetness of a bull in a china shop."

Rich laughter shook Kalilah's shoulders. "I was only stating the obvious, Kai. You were drooling over Tyler the way my teething baby drools."

Kaiya couldn't help laughing. "What did you want to tell me, Lah?"

Kalilah looked away instantly and toyed with a stray balloon in her hands. Her eyes took in a distant gaze for a moment.

"What is it, Lah? You're scaring me," she said and looked around the yard to make sure her daughter was in perfect health condition. She saw the little girl happily playing with her cousins and cuddling them.

Letting out a deep sigh, Kalilah announced, "I invited Mom and Dad to the party."

"What?" Kaiya couldn't believe her ears.

Looking frustrated, Kalilah said, "I'm sorry, Kai. I had to. The twins told me that they wanted their grandparents here, and there was no way I could tell them no since it's their party. I don't like our parents, but the twins love them."

Kaiya understood what her sister just told her. She would have done the same in her shoes. She would most probably do the same if Lili had asked.

"I'm sorry, Kaiya," Kalilah's voice cut into her thoughts.

"It's okay, Lah. I don't blame you. I understand that you had to; after all, they're the twins' grandparents. But I don't want them anywhere near my daughter," she firmly told her sister.

Kalilah sighed loudly, looking remorseful.

"I'm sorry, Lah. We'll just have to leave before they come."

* * *

Tyler took a sip from his beer and nodded at Finn who was handling the grill like a pro. Tyler's gaze kept alternating from his daughter to Kaiya. His woman was looking exceptionally beautiful in a gold sheath dress that did wonderful things to her curves. His hands itched to take off the dress no matter how lovely it was and to see her glorious hair spread across his pillows.

A smile tugged at the corners of his lips as he took in the beautiful scene of children running around, calling to one another and just generally having fun. He laughed as he studied his daughter hitting a piñata shaped like a dinosaur. She kept on hitting it until it finally burst open. The children scampered from all directions to pick the goodies that fell from the torn dinosaur. There was so much exuberance; he couldn't help laughing for a while.

Smiling, he observed as Lili ran to her mom with her goodies, and together, they sorted them out. When Kaiya returned everything to her child, Tyler surmised that none of them contained nuts. Kaiya had been freaking out about Lili mistakenly taking nuts at the party, so much so that Kalilah had called him aside and begged him to talk to Kaiya because she was driving her crazy with her nut-free paranoia. Tyler had laughed at the conversation before proceeding to tell Kaiya to ease off with her worry. Only then had Kaiya relaxed her stance concerning it. And now, seeing Kaiya obviously still worried about it made him smile. She was a wonderful mother.

"You two need to get a room already."

Tyler straightened and turned to see Jalissa presenting him with a knowing look. She must have followed the direction of his gaze and seen it trained on her best friend.

Unable to think of anything witty to reply her, Tyler offered her a small smile. Jalissa took a can of beer from the drum and opened it. After taking a gulp, she stared at him.

"So, you're talking to me again?" he said tentatively, unsure of her reaction since she was still very much loyal to her best friend. Not that he cared, but he didn't like looking like an ogre before her.

She shrugged. "I guess. I'm no longer mad at you."

Tyler let out a deep sigh of relief, and Jalissa laughed.

"No more jabs and threats when you see me?" Tyler asked with mock humility.

Jalissa laughed again. "Of course not." Her face turned serious. "Hurt my friend, and I'll make good on these threats."

"I care too much about her to hurt her, so breathe easy."

Jalissa peered at him intently, as if trying to read his soul. Tyler could understand her concern for her friend. After all, she had always likened them to two peas in a pod. They used to do practically everything together, and he didn't think anything had changed between them. Even though Kaiya had a daughter now, he was sure that Jalissa didn't mind at all. Tyler wished he could have a friend as loyal as Jalissa.

In what seemed like she was overcome by emotion, Jalissa covered the short distance between them and threw her arms around him for a moment before pulling away.

"You're in love with her..."

Her statement stunned him. Was he in love with Kaiya?

Jalissa grinned when he remained silent then walked away. Tyler watched her leave, and his mind remained in turmoil. He took a seat in the wicker chair to go over things in his mind when Finn came up next to him with a plate in hand.

"So, what are your intentions toward my sister-in-law?" Finn asked as he settled on a chair beside Tyler.

Tyler groaned. "Why are you just asking me this?"

The man reclining on the wicker chair beside him sighed and said, "Truthfully, Kalilah made me ask. I would have taken another approach, but I've come to realize that the saying, happy wife, happy life, is indeed true."

Tyler's body shook with laughter.

"What plans do you have for Kaiya?" Finn asked again.

"Kaiya and I are taking things one day at a time."

"Don't hurt her because if you do, it's going to upset Kalilah a lot, which means, I'll be affected, and I don't need a rift between us. I got an earful when you arrived here, and she discovered I was your business partner. So, please don't put me through that again."

Laughing, Tyler nodded and told him he didn't have an intention to hurt Kaiya.

Finn thanked him, and then they focused their attention on the party where the kids were having the time of their lives. Tyler saw Kaiya going into the house. He excused himself and went after her. Ever since they arrived at Finn's place, they hadn't had a moment to themselves.

He grinned when he saw Kaiya head into the washroom. He entered the room close behind her and swirled her around. A little scream of surprise rose in her throat, but he silenced it with a kiss.

Wrenching her lips from his, she hit his chest playfully and laughed. "You scared me."

"Really?" He smiled and drew her closer into his arms. "I thought you heading here was like a signal for me to follow you."

"What?" Laughter burst from her throat. "The thought never crossed my mind."

He cocked his brows with a glint in his eyes. "Are you sure? I could have sworn that I saw you undressing me with these sexy eyes of yours a moment ago."

She shook her head, laughing. "You're incorrigible, Ty."

He threw back his head, and warm laughter tore from his throat. Then his eyes darkened, and his head lowered. Teasingly, he parted Kaiya's lips with his. Her hands instantly went into his hair, caressing and massaging it as she pressed her body against his hard length. His hands reached for her breasts, and he caressed them, flipping his fingers across her rock-hard nipples. Kaiya moaned with pleasure against his lips which were moving demandingly against hers. His tongue pushed apart her lips, diving into her mouth in an erotic dance with her tongue. Her head fell back, and she bit her lip hard when Tyler's mouth replaced his fingers as he sucked her nipples through her dress. Her hand lowered and captured the thick bulge straining his trousers. A loud moan escaped from his lips.

She was already undoing his buckle when they heard a burst of noise outside the door. They both came back to earth instantly and quickly drew apart with labored breaths. Tyler took in deep and slow breaths to bring his heated body back under control. When he felt he had put his desire in order again, he winked at Kaiya.

"I'll be waiting outside."

She nodded without saying a word, her cheeks flushed, and her lips swollen from his kisses. Tyler stepped away from the place and saw several children playing there. As soon as one of them saw him, she smiled at him and then went into the washroom.

Tyler raked his fingers through his hair, feeling like a teenager all over again. He had got carried away by the sight of Kaiya. He would have to find a way to get a control of himself next time. This was a party with kids moving all over the place.

Even though he felt he shouldn't have given in to the urge of wanting to make love so badly to Kaiya, he grinned. He had enjoyed the short make-out session. He was glad that Kaiya was always ready for him. It was a huge turn-on for him.

Whistling softly under his breath, he went to the living room, and thankfully, it was empty. He settled himself on one of the couches in the large space and waited for his woman. She joined him some minutes later, carrying a smile across her beautiful face.

"What?" he questioned as she sat down beside him.

"There's a very inquisitive little girl in the washroom asking all sorts of questions." Kaiya giggled, and the sound sent a warm flush running through him.

Tyler laughed. "What did you tell her?"

"That you lost your way, and I was giving you directions."

They burst into laughter.

"Kalilah told me a moment ago that she invited my parents."

Tyler didn't know what to say to that. Kaiya still didn't want to have anything to do with her parents. He had tried to broker peace between them, particularly her mother, but she refused. It pained him that Lili was missing out on having maternal grandparents, but it was their own doing. He still felt a slight animosity toward Richard for what he did, but now that he had both Kaiya and Lili in his lives, his rage wasn't so intense anymore.

He had waited to see how Richard would carry out the threats he made at the parking lot that day, which his daughter wasn't aware of except for the fact that he had returned the man's money to him. He had thought that Richard would try to sabotage his work at the mall, but Finn had assured him that the man wouldn't dare.

Looking at the anguish on Kaiya's face now as she was evidently recurring the past, Tyler wished that he had at least punched Richard in the face that night at the hospital parking lot. It would take a while for Kaiya to come to terms with what her parents did to her.

He cuddled her in his arms until she insisted on them leaving. They quickly said their goodbyes and had to placate a disappointed Lili by taking her to a pizza hut where she had pizza with her favorite topping and some ice-cream. They also promised her that they would take her to La Ronde during the weekend. Kaiya didn't want to return to the house because she feared that she might continue thinking about her parents, so they went to the park. Later that night, Tyler made slow and passionate love to her.

* * *

Things went smoothly between Tyler, Kaiya, and Lili in the days that followed. They saw each other often between the days they shared with Lili; they shared kisses and made love whenever they could.

Tyler realized that he was falling in love with his ex again, and this time around, it was even more intense. He yearned to be with her every minute of the day. Even as he continued to work on the two sites he was developing, which was coming along nicely, he couldn't get her off his mind. He desired to start anew with Kaiya if she would let him.

Tonight, she was bringing Lili over after her dance class. They had created a routine where Tyler dropped his daughter off at school, his mom would then pick her up from school, and drop her over at Kaiya's dance studio. When Kaiya was done for the day, she would then bring Lili home. Although she had balked at it at first, Kaiya had accepted the house keys he gave to her. She could let herself into the house with Lili. These days, she spent most nights at his home. This made him incredibly happy; happiest he'd been in years.

Tyler decided he couldn't wait to spend some time with the two most important females in his life. He closed from work early and went to pick them from the dance school. They decided they wanted Chinese take-out, so he stopped at a Chinese restaurant and ordered some.

Kaiya and Lili sang Disney princesses' songs on their way home. Tyler smiled all through and begged to be taught.

Lili giggled. "You're gonna have to pay for it, Dad."

Tyler threw up his hand in mock exasperation. "Oh, come on. Help me out here, Kai."

Shrugging, Kaiya said, "I'm sorry; I support my daughter."

Tyler watched with amusement as mother and daughter did a fist bump and spread their hands out in the air, making whooshing sounds.

A small trickle of jealousy went through him at the obvious bonding between the two females. He had been in Lili's life all of eight years, and they didn't have a special handshake.

He killed the feeling instantly, ashamed that it went through him. Kaiya had lost eight years of her daughter's life. Kaiya was making up for it the best way she could.

It upset him a little that Lili had still not started calling her 'Mommy.' Kaiya was still 'Miss Kaiya' to her. He knew it hurt Kaiya a lot, but when he voiced his concerns, she had shrugged it off and told him to give their little girl some time to adjust, and it would come naturally to her. She forbade him from having a discussion with Lili about it.

"I see you two have ganged up against me, but I'm gonna have my revenge soon!" He let out a burst of wicked ominous laughter that had both females giggling. Powerful love for both of them flowed within him.

After they had dinner, they played a game of checkers with Lili, and then it was time for her to go to bed. Kaiya bathed her and told her a bedtime story.

"Goodnight, Daddy. I love you," Lili characteristically said as she did every night.

"Goodnight, Pumpkin. I love you." Tyler placed a kiss on her forehead.

Lili turned to look at Kaiya. "Goodnight, Mommy. I love you. I'm glad you found me."

The breath whizzed out of Tyler at his daughter's words. His eyes misted as he saw tears of joy in Kaiya's eyes.

Kaiya sniffed, vividly trying to hold back her tears. "I love you, too, Baby, and I'm ecstatic that I found you. You've brought a lot of joy into my life. Goodnight, Sweetie."

She threw her arms around her little girl and hugged her tightly as Tyler looked on with a warm smile on his face.

Chapter 15

"I can't believe you want to listen to pop music."

Kaiya laughed at Tyler who shrugged shamelessly and grinned back at her, "And I can't believe you want to listen to heavy metal." They were in Tyler's car, on their way to get furniture for Tyler's house. Lili was with her grandmother today. Kaiya and Tyler got into a playful argument over what radio station to listen to. Tyler wanted one that played pop music while Kaiya wanted to listen to something with a little more base. They playfully argued about it all the way to the store.

The store was massive and from her brief overview, they seemed stocked with everything someone might need when furnishing their home. She was excited. "Joybird?" That was the manufacturing info of the office chair they were looking at.

She smiled, "I mean, who doesn't feel instantaneous happiness when they're sitting on furniture from Joybird, it's scientifically proven." Tyler let out a laugh as he settled into an office chair to test it out.

He tapped the arm of the chair he was sitting on and swirled around like Lili would. She pushed him, "Stop playing little boy. We have important grown up shopping to do?"

Tyler guffawed, "Let me show you the little boy." He made to grab her hand, but she darted out of the way. Grinning, he ran after her, they darted in between closets and ducked under furniture before entering the bedroom section and collapsing on a king-sized bed.

Kaiya bounced once for good measure and smiled, "It looks steady. It should withstand Lili's bouncing and her play fights."

"And everything else in between," Tyler raised his eyebrows. He pulled her closer to him and kissed her hard. Kaiya forgot where she was and rolled unto Tyler, straddling his lap, without breaking the connection of their lips. The sound of someone coughing brought back their awareness. They looked into each other's eyes and smiled.

Tyler called out to a store attendant and asked for the bed to be marked for them. The attendant blushed at the sight of them in a compromising position and Tyler winked at her.

Kaiya stood up from the bed and smoothed out her clothes, attempting to get some sort of decorum into her appearance while Tyler lay on the bed smiling at her. She leveled him with a look.

"I've been thinking of getting some bunk beds for when the kids stay over my place. I should get it now."

"Let's go get it."

They were walking through the children's section when her phone beeped, she took it out and sighed, putting it back in her purse. It beeped again and she ignored it. Tyler gave her a suspicious look, "You're not going to get that?"

She sighed, staring at her phone with an angry look as she tapped away at the screen with anger while she spoke to Tyler. "It's the real estate agent for the dance school. He's telling me now that the building has problems. I don't feel like dealing with it now."

He dragged her into a chair and sat beside her, "What problems?"

"Remember I told you about opening a second location for my dance school, well apparently, the building only very narrowly passed inspections and it looks like the structural integrity has been compromised. I honestly don't know what to do. It was the perfect place for the second location and now it looks like it's gonna be way more things to deal with."

Tyler took her hand and squeezed it as she continued talking, "And I really just want to get this school up and running. My grand opening is in three months and it's stressing me out."

She took a deep breath, raising a hand to her temples to massage it. Tyler kissed her knuckles before he started talking, "I can go to the building with you and we can come up with something. I could also look around for other buildings that will suit your needs."

Kaiya could hear him, but she wasn't really processing what he was saying, she was lost in her thoughts, thinking of solutions. She whipped out her phone and dialed Finn's number, waiting for him to pick up.

The call went through and she nearly shouted into the phone, "Finn! Thank God I got you. Marcus said the building had problems and I really can't wrap my head around it. Can you find out what's really going on?" She paused to listen to him before nodding, "Yeah thanks. That'd be great. I owe you one."

She hung up and looked up to see Tyler giving her a dirty look.

"What?"

He shrugged in response and stood up to get their purchases in order. After finalizing the delivery days and times for the purchases they left the store, with none of the jubilance they had when they entered. Even when they were in the car on their way home, Tyler barely said a word to her, not even when she changed the radio station. She couldn't think of anything that could've made him upset.

Did he somehow conclude that her real estate agent – Marcus was her friend with benefits?

The car approached her condo building and before she could ask him to come inside, he told her goodbye.

Kaiya couldn't wrap her head around why he got so distant. In her mind everything was going well. She thought she needed to call the only expert on men she knew.

Jalissa.

Jalissa picked up her phone immediately like she always did, "Hey Kai, what's up?" It was like she pushed a button – Kaiya poured out everything that had happened that afternoon between she and Tyler.

She heard the sound of a scuffle and a new voice sounded in her ears,

"Hello Kaiya. I couldn't help but overhear your conversation with Jal and I hope you don't mind my two cents." Justin? Kaiya wasn't even shocked that Justin was with Jalissa. She learned from Kalilah that Justin spent most of his weekends in Montreal, even though he lives in Ottawa. Jalissa still kept mum about their relationship and Kaiya didn't want to push her friend. She would wait until Jalissa was ready to share.

"Go ahead Justin."

"Tyler is your man and he was right there with you and instead of leaning on him for advice, you called another man for help instead."

Kaiya was beginning to feel horrible. "It was only Finn."

"No man wants to see their woman asking someone else for help when they're right there."

Kaiya shook her head before remembering that they couldn't see her, "But I meant no harm and Finn is my brother in law. There's absolutely no reason for him to feel off, I just felt Finn would be in a better position to help."

"Look at it this way. You're Lili's mom, right? Imagine she had a dance routine to perfect and she went to someone else to help her."

The thought caused a bitter taste in her mouth and she swallowed. She felt immediately guilty. She didn't want Tyler to feel unappreciated.

"Thanks you two, I need to talk to Tyler now. By the way, don't forget to use protection." She hung up before either one could say something.

She dialed Tyler's number while pacing around the house, trying to calm her heart down. Her call went straight to his voicemail and she ended the call. She sent him a quick text.

She dropped her phone and proceeded to pace even more. When she thought time had passed and he didn't return her calls, she called him again. She kept getting his voice message and it started to feel like déjà vu. Her heart sank.

* * *

Tyler was alone in the house, in the silence and it seemed like his thoughts took pleasure in tormenting him. It had been a two days since he had seen Kaiya and he was feeling the pain as acutely as one would feel the pain from the loss of a limb. He had listened to all the voicemails and read all of the text messages she left, yet whenever he wanted to call her, anger would encompass his mind and he'd put the phone down.

He heard the front door slam shut and bolted out of his seat. No one was supposed to be in the house, he reached for the baseball bat he kept behind his door and held his phone in his other hand.

He heard footsteps heading up to his office and he gripped his bat even harder with his heart beating faster as the footsteps slowed in front of his door. In a second the door had flown open and he had raised his bat when there was a scream.

The adrenaline wore off as he recognized Kaiya's voice. She leveled him with a glare, "Are you crazy? What the hell do you think you're doing?"

Her tone made him agitated, "Am I crazy? Are you crazy? You just barged in here. I thought you were a burglar! What if I had a gun? Whatever happened to calling? Or ringing the doorbell? Or knocking?!"

She opened her mouth, presumably to shout before sighing and speaking in a calmer voice, "You've been avoiding my calls," his guilt increased.

He sighed and dropped his baseball bat and pulled her into his arms, missing the feel of her in his arms. She stayed there for a second before pushing him, her anger returning to her face, "Don't think you can distract me Mister, you've been avoiding me and I want to know why."

"I hate this stupid distance between us, it's killing me and you look terrible so it must be killing you too." He smiled at that, remembering how bold she used to be when they were younger, full of fire and never taking no for an answer.

She glared at him, "Don't try using your pretty face to distract me. I'm trying to apologize here. I'm sorry I went to Finn when you were right there. I thought since Finn was Marcus' boss, it'd be easier to handle."

He frowned, remembering how her face looked whenever she said the name 'Marcus', "Is he the same man from the gala?" he asked and he watched an unfamiliar expression flit across her face.

She took a deep breath, "Yes he is," she looked at the ceiling as if to ask for answers before continuing, "Marcus and I used to be involved but now it's simply business. He is nobody important, he never was." Anger took over him at the thought of another man touching and kissing what he considered to be his.

He raised his eyebrows. "Does he know that?"

"I don't care what he knows. Can you please take my word for it? I really don't want to talk about it anymore."

Her face was open, begging him to believe her and he smiled softly, dropping the subject. He took her hands and led her to his computer, he sat in his chair and then pulled her unto his lap. He maneuvered his hands around her to operate the computer.

He clicked on an icon and the 3d model of a building popped up. She gasped and he relished that sound, "Wow, what's that?"

"Your new school babe."

"What? How? When? Who did this?"

"I spent all days yesterday and today working on it. I spoke to Finn and on yours orders, we can demolish the building you bought and rebuild this. What do you think?"

"You did this for me?" She turned her tearful eyes towards him.

"I did. I want you to know that you can come to me for anything, Kai. I'll do anything to put a smile on your pretty face."

"I love it Ty. When can we make this building a reality?

"We can start demolishing the building in two days and have your new building started within a week."

"Aww thanks Ty. I really appreciate this. You're an amazing architect." She placed kisses all over his face and he bit the tip of her nose.

She laughed, the sound making his head lighter and his loins tightened in response. He took a deep breath to get himself in order before speaking, "I'm really sorry about the distance between us."

"I forgive you," she said with a laugh.

He turned back to the computer and started describing each feature of her dance school. "I designed each room with floor to ceiling windows so they could see the outside and feel the beauty from outside and within, adagio floors, mirrors and soundproof walls."

He finished in a rush and she turned to face him, straddling him and kissing his lips with full force. He kissed her back just as fiercely.

146

He hoisted her up on his body and stood up with intentions of getting to his bedroom —relying more memory than sight. He climbed up the stairs with ease then bumped into the side of the door and they broke the kiss to laugh. She attached her lips on his again and they finally made it to the bed where he loved her all night.

* * *

A few days later, Kaiya was babysitting her niece and nephew. Lili had been with her for the past two days since Tyler was very busy with overseeing the building of her new dance studio in addition to the mall site. She had had a very busy day with them and was glad that they were all asleep.

She walked down to the room where Lili, Max, and Millie were sleeping. She fixed their covers, and emotion tugged at her heart again at how cute they all looked on their beds. She thanked the stars again that she bought the bunk beds when she did. If she hadn't, the children would have had to share her old queen-sized bed.

She walked over to the small cot where Myles slept and caressed his chubby cheek. She wondered again if she should move his cot to her bedroom and decided that she would to be on the safe side.

Finn had brought the cot earlier and Kalilah was adamant that Myles now slept through the night. She was glad about that even though she knew she would check on them throughout the night.

Sighing, she left the room and shut the door slightly behind her. She was walking towards her room when she heard the buzzer. Her heart pounded against her chest hoping that the sound wouldn't wake the children.

Who could that be? She didn't expect any guests tonight. Her sister would have called before coming over.

Nervously, she walked to the door, certain that Tyler was the one standing at the other side of it. Her breath whooshed out of her when she saw through the peephole that he was indeed the one. A thrill went through her as it always

147

did whenever she set eyes on the handsome hunk of a man.

She took a moment to compose herself and bring her heightened color back to normal before opening the door.

"Tyler," she called in a rather high pitch. "I didn't think I would see you tonight."

Her lips became dry when Tyler didn't say anything but gave her a searing look. That was when she realized that she was still on her towel, which was displaying portions of her breasts and a fair amount of her legs since it ended way above her knees.

She felt Tyler shedding the piece of material off her body. Her body tightened, her nipples became rock hard, and she felt moisture in her core.

Clearing her throat, she dashed the tip of her tongue across her lips and asked him to come in.

When the door shut behind him without breaking eye contact, he asked in a hoarse voice, "Where's Lili and her cousins?"

Stepping back a little, Kaiya answered, "They're all asleep. Thank God."

Tyler grinned and pulled her towards him and kissed her fiercely.

Elevating his head, he said, "I missed you and couldn't stop thinking about you for the past few days."

"Oh." Joy flowed within her.

Tyler whispered against her lips. "I think we should take this to the shower since you were heading there anyway."

Kaiya gave him a dazzling smile picked up the baby monitor before leading the way. She helped Tyler strip off his clothes, and they went into the bathroom together. Kaiya placed the baby monitor on her vanity. After stepping into the shower and turned on the faucet. Tyler picked up the soap and rubbed it all over her breasts.

She gasped at the sensations moving all over her body as he circled her hardened nipples with the soap and the warm spray bathed them.

He dropped the soap and grabbed her breasts, kneading them, making her tilt her head back as she bit her lip in enjoyment. Then she reached forward and grabbed his manhood, massaging it also in rhythm with her breasts.

Tyler's hand trailed down her body to cup her moist center, and he inserted a finger into it. Kaiya jerked as he began to stroke her clitoris.

A low moan fell from Kaiya's throat as her hand tautened on his shaft. Tyler worked on her breast with one hand and her clitoris with his other hand until spasms got her jerking as she found her release in a matter of minutes.

Grinning, he turned off the shower, and Kaiya went down on him, taking his rigid length into her mouth and sucking on it until he begged her to stop.

He lifted her, turned her around, placed her hands on the shower knobs, and inclined her body in such a way that she would receive his thrusts deeply into her moist center.

Kaiya cried with ecstasy when he slid into her from behind. He went slowly into her at first, and then the pressure increased as he thrust in and out of her, fast and hard.

Her legs began to wobble from the intensity of his thrusts. Tyler changed positions and brought her down to her knees, thrusting in and out of her.

Kaiya cried out in mindless passion as convulsions took over her body, and she found her release. Tyler came with her, and together, they crumbled on the floor of the cubicle.

"With you, it gets better every time," he murmured into her ears, making her blush.

After they caught their breaths, they rose to take a shower, which ended in another bout of lovemaking before they actually took a shower. Tyler toweled Kaiya dry and took her to the bedroom where they made love all night long.

As they did the other night, they rose early to avoid questions from the children. Tyler thought it was best if he showered alone, so nothing would delay him from leaving her room. Giggling, she nodded.

Tyler came out of her bathroom some minutes later with a towel barely covering his torso, leaving his muscular chest and six-packs stomach bare for her to ogle. Kaiya couldn't believe that after making love with him all night, the mere sight of his half-naked body was making her mouth run dry and her vagina to grow moist. Embarrassed that she couldn't get enough of him, she rushed out of the room to the bathroom to turn the shower into a cold blast to cool her heated body.

When she came out of the bathroom a short while later, it was to see Tyler standing beside one of her drawers gawking at his grandmother's necklace he had given her so long ago.

Her face reddened when he lifted his head to regard her with a questioning gaze.

"I didn't mean to snoop. I was looking for a comb."

She nodded, wishing the ground would open up and swallow her.

"I can't believe this. You kept it?"

She shrugged, trying to make light of it. "It was too beautiful for me to throw it out. I just couldn't do it. Besides, I didn't think I had the right to throw it out since you said it was your grandmother's and...and..." She bit her lip and stared down at her bare feet. "It was the only thing I thought I had left of you..."

With an intense emotion that she couldn't read, Tyler hurried to her and placed the necklace around her neck. He gave her a kiss that made her forget everything else. After the kiss ended, she asked Tyler to spend the night and he agreed. Before falling asleep, Tyler moved Myles' cot into their bedroom so that they could attend to the baby's need during the night if necessary. They both fell into a relaxed slumber holding each other close.

Fortunately for them, the children were still asleep when they were finally able to drag themselves away from her bed early the next day to prepare breakfast.

"Can I ask you something?" Tyler asked suddenly as he whisked the eggs for the kids' breakfast.

"Sure, go ahead."

"How come you never fulfilled your dreams of becoming a professional ballerina?" His question caused her to pause from placing the first scoop of blueberry pancakes on the skillet. Probably seeing the sadness on her face he quickly added, "You don't need to answer if you don't want to, I am just curious, since you were one of the best – still the best dancer in my opinion."

"It's okay that you asked. After thinking that our baby died, I didn't feel the same excitement I once felt for professional ballet." She believed that because she wished their baby away in the beginning of her pregnancy because of her professional ballet dreams, she didn't deserve to live out that dream. "I blamed myself for the loss of our child. I didn't think I deserved to live out my dreams while our baby was dead and had no future." Tears threatened to pool her eyes, but she held them at bay.

Tyler placed the bowl which held the egg mixture down and moved over to where she stood and wrapped his arms around her. She breathed in his scent and allowed his strength to seep through her soul, while he rubbed her back with his hand.

"I'm sorry Kai. Even though our child wouldn't have survived, it wouldn't have been your fault. You were young, remember? Having dreams and ambitions are okay. They don't cause babies to die. Besides, everything that happened is my fault. I was older and knew the consequences of unprotected sex. If I never..."

She cut him off before he could finish. "Stop! You're only a year older than I am. We both knew the consequences of unprotected sex and took the risk anyway. If we took the necessary precautions, our Lili wouldn't exist." "I know and I can't regret you getting pregnant. I just wish I could change the circumstances. I wish I was there." She saw the guilt in his eyes and wished to reassure him that it wasn't his fault, but knew he needed to come to that conclusion on his own.

"I feel the same way, Hon. Ty, I just couldn't move on with my life knowing our baby was dead. I spent a great deal of years after giving birth in therapy for my anxiety and depression. Until Kalilah returned and forced me out of my shell, I lived on autopilot. I didn't care about anything except getting through the minutes in a day. Thankfully, our child is alive and healthy."

Tyler broke away from their embrace but kept his hands on her arms. He looked directly at her and said, "I'm sorry for everything you went through. I wish I could wrap my hands around your dad's neck."

"Join the club!" She reached up and place a soft kiss on his cheek, then stepped out of his hold and resumed making her pancakes. She still didn't understand her dad's thought process and she didn't want to understand it either. She was done with Richard Anderson. The parenting books she read while pregnant, always mentioned that the first two years of a child's life was the most important period for parents to form a secure attachment to a child.

This type of attachment is supposed to build strong bonds between parents and children that would last a lifetime. She wasn't given that opportunity to bond with her child. She wanted to do everything in her power to form that bond with her child now, since she was late in parenthood and at a disadvantage. Building a secure and solid bond with her daughter was all that mattered to her.

"I wish things could have been different for us, but I'm happy you've been reunited with our daughter. I'm even happier to be reunited with you."

"Me too Ty." She smiled in his direction and watched as he poured the eggs into a frying pan. She flipped another pancake and then heard tiny footsteps coming towards the kitchen. The big kids were finally awake, and she couldn't be any happier than she is now. A month ago, she would have never imaged that this would be her life. She wouldn't have it any other way.

Chapter 16

"Mommy, take a look at what I drew," Lili called to her mom the following day.

Kaiya wondered if she would ever get used to Lili calling her 'Mommy.' They were words she thought she would never be called. Even though she loved children to a distraction, getting pregnant again was out of her plans. She had feared that what happened with her supposed dead son wasn't a one-off thing and that it would continue happening, shattering her heart.

Kaiya left her painting to look at that of her daughter's. She saw that Lili had painted four people. Three of them looked like Kaiya, Tyler, and Lili. She couldn't decipher who the fourth person was. Could it be Max or Millie? Why not draw both of them?

Munching on a piece of the cake that her mom bought on their way to her house, Lili explained her drawing.

"That's Daddy, you, me, and my baby brother."

Kaiya's eyes misted. Lili wanted them to be a complete family. She desperately wanted that too, but it was up to Tyler. Even though things had been going steady with them, Lili's father hadn't given any indication that he wanted things taken to the next level.

"Thanks, sweetie." Kaiya hugged her daughter and took a piece of the cake.

Kaiya cocked her head to the side when she thought she tasted something like nuts in it. She had specifically told the salesgirl that she wanted a nut-free cake.

Kaiya's suspicions were proven right when she saw her daughter turning blue in the face. Lili began to gasp for air, and her mom screamed.

"Lili!"

She shook her daughter and tried to remove the remnants of the cake from her mouth. Completely freaked out as her daughter continued to fight for air, she looked around for her phone.

"Dear God, Please. Dear God, Please. Please don't take my daughter away from me. Not now that I just found her."

Tears poured down her face in waves. Carrying her daughter in her arms, all the while weeping, she went to her living room and retrieved her phone from the coffee table.

"Tyler! I don't know what went wrong. Lili is gasping for air. I think there were nuts in the cake I bought."

Calmly Tyler replied, "Use her EpiPen. It's inside her backpack."

Laying her daughter gently on the couch, Kaiya ran to get the backpack and found the pen after unzipping the bag, almost ruining it in her haste. She stumbled as she ran back to the living room where her poor daughter was still gasping for breath.

"What do I do?" she yelled into the phone.

Still in a calm voice, Tyler explained, "You need to make sure the orange tip is pointing downward, pull out the safety cap, and place the orange tip against the middle of her thigh."

Kaiya, with her hands visibly shaking, did all that Tyler said. "What next?" she shouted hastily.

"Now, push the auto-injector into her thigh until it clicks."

Kaiya nearly shouted for joy when she heard the click sound.

"Hold it down for three seconds. Count slowly."

With tears still rolling down her eyes, Kaiya did just that and breathed a sigh of relief when a moment later, Lili started breathing normally again, even though she looked very pale and weak.

"Call 911. I'll meet you at the hospital."

Kaiya ended the call and quickly called 911. Then she took her daughter into her arms and continued weeping and apologizing.

"I'm so sorry. I'm so sorry."

"It's okay, Mommy. You didn't know," Lili said weakly in her mother's arms.

"I should have checked to make sure. I should have asked the salesgirl if the cake was indeed nut-free. After making sure everything at the twins' party was nut-free, I can't believe I was so careless about the cake."

Kaiya continued crying and blaming herself. She couldn't believe she almost lost her daughter due to her ineptitude. She cuddled the little girl to herself until she had to leave her to go and open the door for the paramedics.

She followed in the ambulance, holding her daughter's hand and praying she would be alright and have no lasting effect from the allergic reaction.

Tyler came to meet her while she was waiting in the reception area. She rushed into his arms and burst into tears.

"I'm so sorry. I'm so sorry," she chanted, weeping.

Tyler hushed her. "It's okay, Kai. Don't get yourself worked up over it. Accidents happen."

Kaiya shook her head. "I should have known better."

"No, Kaiya. Stop punishing yourself. It happens. It has happened a number of times. You can't always be sure. All you can do is your best. So don't beat yourself so much about it, okay?"

Kaiya cried on heedlessly until the doctor came out and told her that her daughter was okay but would have to stay a few days for monitoring. Kaiya was relieved to hear that even though she still blamed herself for the incident.

She hugged her daughter fiercely when they were allowed to see her. She kept asking the little girl to forgive her.

Tyler rolled his eyes. "Kai, she has already said you don't have to apologize like a hundred times. She's fine."

"You don't understand." Kaiya sniffed. "I came this close to losing her."

His features softened. "I understand, Kai, that it has brought back unpleasant memories, but thank God she's okay now."

Kaiya nodded and struggled to pull herself together. Indeed it brought back painful memories, but this was a different scenario altogether. She kissed her daughter's hand and smiled at her.

Kalilah and her family came to visit when they learned of the incident. After that, Kaiya and her sister made sure their homes were nut-free.

Kaiya remained glued to her daughter's side for the next few days. Even though the doctor told her that Lili was okay now, Kaiya refused to leave her daughter's side, ensuring that she was well-rested even when they got home.

"Kaiya," Tyler whispered by the door.

Kaiya turned to look at him. She placed a finger on her lips to tell him to keep silent and pointed at their sleeping daughter. He beckoned on her to come to him. Reluctantly, she cast a look at her daughter and rose from the chair beside the bed which she had sat on for days.

Tyler took her hand when she reached the door and practically dragged her out of the room.

"I've told Mom to look after Lili. We're going dancing," he firmly told her in a tone that brooked no argument.

But Kaiya, being stubborn, placed her hands on her hips and glared at him. "How can you possibly think of going dancing when our little girl is lying in there?"

"She's not sick. Neither is she dying. Three days ago, she was certified fit by the doctor, but for some reason, you didn't seem to hear that bit and have been mollycoddling her ever since."

Although his tone was light, and she knew he was teasing, she felt slighted. She folded her arms across her chest.

"What would she think if she woke up sometime in the night and discover that we'd gone dancing?"

"Probably shout Alleluia." He chuckled. "For three nights, you have watched her sleep. How many times did she wake up?"

Kaiya stared at her shoe and drew circles with it on the carpet.

"Kaiya, Lili is fine. I love the fact that you're so sweet and caring toward her, but you must realize that you can't spend the rest of your life and hers beside her bed."

Acknowledging that he was right, she reluctantly nodded. "I'll text Jalissa to bring me some dancing clothes."

"Atta girl!" Tyler said excitedly and dragged her into his arms to give her a kiss.

The kiss got heated because they hadn't had the opportunity to be together since Kaiya had been fastened to their daughter's side for days.

"You two should get a room."

An amused voice got them jolting apart and looking guilty like two teenagers caught smooching.

Tyler's mom gave them a knowing look with a smile puckering her lips. Tyler muttered something incoherent and left the two women.

Kaiya cleared her throat, grateful that she finally had a chance to talk to the woman who mostly kept to herself or was out visiting friends.

"I've never had the opportunity of thanking you for being there for Lili all these years. Thank you," Kaiya said with heartfelt gratitude.

Smiling, the woman covered the distance between them and took her hand. "And I thank you for coming into her life. Grandma can only do so much. After Lena's death, I knew she needed her mother. I'm so sorry for what you went through. I hope being with her makes up for it."

Smiling through her tears, Kaiya nodded. "It sure does."

The two women hugged and went to check on Lili together. Jalissa delivered the clothing and warned her not to have too much fun considering how fertile she was. They both laughed at that.

Kaiya felt very sexy in the black short flared leather dress her best friend brought for her. She teamed it with knee-length leather boots and let her hair down just the way Tyler liked it.

Tyler whistled when he saw her. He, too, looked drop-dead gorgeous in a polo shirt, jeans, and sneakers.

"The night might end in a brawl if a man so much as whistles at you let alone touches you on the dance floor."

Kaiya giggled. She felt so alive; she wanted to yell it for all and sundry to hear. Tyler asked her to do just that on their way to the club. He opened the car's roof. Kaiya stood up, threw her arms in the air with the wind blowing her hair about, and screamed, "I'm alive!"

Tyler laughed heartily inside the car.

She and Tyler hit the club, and she felt like she was back again to her teenage years when she'd just met Tyler. They had a nice time dancing the whole night away.

Kaiya was surprised that instead of heading home, Tyler pulled up in the parking lot of an exclusive hotel. When she wanted to protest about Lili, he reminded her that his mom was with their little girl and had spent many a night with her when she was sick.

Giggling, Kaiya felt like a teenage girl sneaking off to go and make love with her boyfriend. They were so hot for each other that they couldn't keep their hands off each other in the elevator. They didn't make it to the bed when they got to the hotel room. Later, Tyler made slow and passionate love to Kaiya, which left her so contented; she never wanted them to leave the place.

"This might be very inappropriate, but I really need to know about your relationship with Lena. I know now that you never cheated on me with her, but I just want to know what happened with her," Kaiya said into the comfortable silence that fell between them.

Exhaling softly, Tyler said, "Lena was a lesbian."

"Say what now?"

"That was one of the reasons she became super clingy then. She was still trying to come to terms with it, and it frightened her immensely. She was also dealing with nightmares of her childhood, where her stepfather repeatedly abused her with her drug addict mother doing little or nothing about it. When her mother died from drug overdose, she ran away from home, knowing her fate would be worse in the hands of her stepfather. So, she was constantly troubled by it. I'm happy that having Lili in her life gave her a new lease on life. She became such a devoted mother that all her ghosts were laid to rest. It's a pity death took her away from us. She was a wonderful person who you would have gotten along with but for your suspicions. You know, you both look alike in a lot of ways."

Kaiya chewed the inside of her cheek as regret over the way she had treated the disturbed girl and had wished many evil things on her because she felt she had stolen Tyler from her.

"I could relate with what she went through because just as her mom was a drug addict, mine was an alcoholic and depressed. She became that way because my father was married to someone else when he got her pregnant.

She thought he would leave his wife for her. When he didn't, she fell into depression and turned to alcohol for solace. I have two older brothers from my father's side that I know nothing about. I don't know their names or what they do.

Just like Lena, growing up in group homes wasn't easy. I never told you this, but I was physically abused by one of my mother's boyfriends."

"Oh, God!" Kaiya's hand went to her mouth as she fought to hold back her tears.

"I was about eight, I think. He broke my arm and a few ribs. I spent an entire month at the hospital."

"I'm so sorry, Ty." She placed a kiss on his cheeks.

Shrugging against the headboard, he said, "It doesn't matter anymore. All that is in the past now."

A cloak of silence fell between them.

"Ty, have you ever wondered how it would have been between us if my dad hadn't interfered in our lives?"

Tyler let out a loud sigh. "I think of it sometimes and regret that we never got the chance to know."

"Me too. Do you think we would have still been together?"

He looked contemplative before he answered. "I believe we would still be together. I loved you so much back then and having our daughter would have made that love stronger."

Kaiya bit her bottom lip. "Are you sure? We were pretty young, and the pressure of raising a child at such an age might have taken its toll on us."

Tyler gave her an incredulous look.

She shrugged. "I'm just trying to look at it from another point of view. What if I hadn't gotten pregnant with Lili? Would we have made it as a couple?"

Tyler cradled her face. "What if I never got into business with Finn? What if my mom never registered Lili for dance classes at your school? I don't like this what-if game. I like to believe that what we feel for each other is everlasting and transcends everything. I love you, Kaiya, and no matter what was put in our path, we would always end up back together. I want to be with you forever if you let me."

"I want to be with you forever, Ty. I love you, too."

"You're not just saying it for Lili's sake, are you?"

Giggling, she shook her head. "I loved you before I loved Lili. I love you now more than I loved you then. In fact, I don't think I ever stopped loving you."

"I don't think I fell out of love with you either. I didn't remove Lili from your dance class because deep down, I think I wanted you to fall in love with her and realize that she wasn't a mistake and that we belonged with you - together as a family."

She kissed him. A slow kiss.

"Lili has never been a mistake."

He nodded. "You mean the world to me, and I'm so glad we found each other again."

They discussed their future together in between bouts of lovemaking. Tyler asked her to move in with him and she agreed almost immediately. She would move in by the end of the month. Tyler had asked if she wanted to move to a new house or neighborhood and she declined. She liked Tyler's house and besides, she picked out most of the furniture in the house. There were enough bedrooms in the house for them to expand on their family if they were so inclined.

"What about my mom? She occupies my basement. It's renovated into a full apartment for her needs. And I'm afraid that..."

She knew he was worried about her sobriety and all the changes that have taken place in the last few months. "It's okay, she doesn't have to move out. Your house is big enough for us all."

"She's spent most of her sobriety caring for Lili and for me."

"Ty, you don't have to explain. I really like your mom. On the occasions I went by your place, she spent most of her time running errands or stayed in her own apartment. I don't mind your mom living below us." Kaiya meant it too.

"Have I told you that you're the most incredible woman I know?"

"You have, but one can never tire of hearing how incredible they are."

"Well I've always been better at showing than I am at telling." After that proclamation, he caught one of her nipples in his mouth and spent the rest of the night showing her exactly how incredible she is.

* * *

A week later...

"Hi, Erin. Thanks so much for meeting with me." Tyler rose from his chair, reached out, and shook hands with the smiling woman who just approached the table.

"You're welcome, Tyler," Erin returned and settled on the opposite chair in the fancy dining room. "And you don't have to keep on thanking me."

Given the circumstance, it was the least he could do. Erin had shown that she was a very understanding woman. When he had told his colleague that he was planning a surprise event for his girlfriend, the man had suggested his sister handling it. Tyler had felt it would be awkward since Erin had wanted them to date. His colleague had told him his sister wasn't like that. Besides, she had moved on, and there was another man on the horizon. That convinced him to call her about the surprise party he wanted for Kaiya.

"Things don't have to be awkward between us, Tyler. This is business. Although things didn't work out between us, I understood that Lili needed her mom as a permanent figure in her life," she had informed him even before they began. And with a twinkle in her eyes, she had said, "Besides, I noticed how sparks flew between you and Kaiya." Sighing, she added, "I can't compete with that."

Tyler had marveled at how considerate she was and had thanked her for being very understanding. And so, he hired her for the surprise party and catering the dinner for Kaiya's engagement party.

"Everything is set for tonight, Tyler. You don't have to worry about anything. Everything that might have been a source of concern to you has all been sorted out. All you have to do is bring your queen to the venue and make sure she doesn't have an inkling of what's going on."

"Believe me, she has no idea. Everyone has been sworn to secrecy."

Erin nodded as a bright smile spanned across her face. "Oh, I do so love surprise parties."

Tyler grinned. The hotel where the surprise engagement party was to take place wasn't too far from his workplace, and because his event was such short notice, he had Finn call in some favors for him. He needed tonight to be perfect.

He relayed the message to the event planner. "I really need tonight to be perfect."

"Don't worry, it will be," she promised solemnly. Opening the portfolio she brought along with her, she said, "Let's go through the details again to set your mind at ease."

Chapter 17

Kaiya had never been so bored. She couldn't understand what was happening to her. This was a career she loved so much, nothing else mattered. But now, as she walked about listlessly in the dancing hall, she couldn't wait to see Tyler and her daughter again.

Even though they had all been together that morning, having a long breakfast at Tyler's place, she missed them terribly. She knew they had their own lives to live, but it didn't stop her from yearning to be with them every minute of the day.

Then she remembered that in a few hours, they would all be together again. Tyler had suggested that they should eat out at a fancy restaurant that night, and she had obliged.

"What did I do with my life before they came into it?" she giggled as she asked herself.

Since she was in such a good mood because her business was thriving, her second studio was coming together thanks to Tyler's help, and now, she was reunited with the man she loved and the child she thought she had lost forever. Kaiya burst into a dance.

Extremely excited to start her life anew again with everyone she loved in it, she continued dancing. There wasn't any music playing in the background, but a melodious tune she loved so much rang in her head, and she danced to it for some minutes.

On the home front, her parents had also reconciled, and they had been asking if they could spend some time with Lili. Kaiya was totally against it. They gave up that right when they gave up her child without her knowledge.

"They seemed genuinely sorry for their actions." Tyler told her two days ago.

He would know because her father had astonishingly reached out to Tyler. Kaiya had a feeling that her mom was behind her dad's efforts. Her dad had called him out of the blue and invited him over. Kaiya had begged him not to go because it might be a trap. Tyler had laughed and told her to stop reading mystery novels. She knew deep down that he also wanted the opportunity to finally confront her father.

The man she loved had gone for the meeting and returned in one piece and in good spirits. According to him, her father had apologized for what he did years ago and asked for peace to reign between them. Her father also asked that Tyler talk Kaiya into meeting with them so they could apologize.

"You told him to go to hell, didn't you?' Kaiya had questioned him with her hands akimbo. She wasn't ready to hear or accept apologies. What her father did to her couldn't be fixed with an apology. Her mom failing to tell her the truth couldn't be fixed with an apology either.

Tyler had laughed and drawn her resistant body into his arms.

"I wanted to, but I didn't. I did tell him that his place in our lives depended on you. If you are not okay with him being in our daughter's life, then I'll respect your decision. It's up to you, babe. You and Lili were the ones hurt the most from his decisions."

"You trust my decision on this?"

"Yes, I do, babe, whatever you decide. We can even move to another Province if you want to."

She had laughed at that. "We don't have to move, but I'm not ready to forgive them." Her parents had tried to reach out to her multiple times, but she was still not ready to talk to them. She'd grown close to her mom after she lost her child and that's why her betrayal hurt most. "Taking my child from me and having me believe that *he* was dead for year is going to far. I may forgive them one day, but for now..."

He had kissed her then to silence her, and the kiss sent shock waves throughout her body, and her mind forgot everything else.

"Can I ask you something Ty?" She asked after putting an end to their kiss.

"What is it? This better be good since you broke our kiss."

"Do you still feel guilty about getting me pregnant?" He tried capturing her lips again, but she placed her hand between their lips.

"That was mean."

"I know. Now answer my question."

"I still do sometimes, especially when I'm reminded or think of how much you suffered during and after the pregnancy."

"I told you already that you're not at fault. Anyway, I wanna make a deal..."

"Sure, as long as we can get back to our prior activity." He winked.

"I will hear my parents out when you no longer feel guilty about Lili's birth and my recovery."

"You don't play fair, babe." She really didn't. She knew how much he wanted her to forgive her parents so that they could start their lives together with no past bitterness.

"I know."

"Deal!" He said before he swept her in his arms again and kissed her.

Smiling at what a wonderful person Tyler was, she stopped dancing. He could have insisted that she cut her parents off and have nothing to do with them, but instead, he was giving her the choice and open to her reconciling with them. She really didn't want to hold a grudge against her parents forever. She had held a grudge against Tyler, and it brought her nothing but pain and anger.

Thinking of what a great man Tyler was, she decided to surprise him at work during lunch break. It was almost lunchtime, and he would be delighted to see her.

Changing out of her dance clothes into a floral dress, she walked out of the dance studio. These days, she no longer favored sweatshirts and leggings. Tyler loved seeing her in dresses, and so she had gone shopping with Jalissa. Her hair was now perpetually loose across her back except when she was teaching or doing chores. Anything to please the man she loved.

The smile on her face turned into a frown when she got to the job site and was told that he had already gone out to lunch.

Crestfallen because she just missed him, she left the place and slowly walked out. The thought of eating alone wasn't appealing to her, so she decided that she would just make herself a sandwich when she got back to the office.

Kaiya's eyes nearly pooped out of their sockets when a few meters down the road, she spotted Tyler walking out of a hotel with Erin.

Her heart sank to her feet with a loud thud when she saw Erin lean into Tyler and laughed heartily at something he said.

Oh, he wasn't only a cheat but a comedian as well?

Anger surged through her at his duplicity. How could he do this to her? How could he do this to them? She had foolishly thought things were going smoothly for them. Her mind had hoped that in the near future, they would make their relationship official and maybe expand on their family.

"How foolish of me!"

The man was only interested in having sex with her. Why he had felt the need to profess a fake love for her was beyond her. Maybe he got high just knowing that she loved him when it wasn't reciprocated. Perhaps it was just a revenge plot of his that he had to carry out even though the truth had come out about her innocence.

Oh, she had the mind of pulling over, going to him, and giving him a piece of her mind. She would tell him never to come near her again. Since they still had their daughter between them, she would find a way for her to be with the little girl without seeing him. It would break the little girl's heart that things didn't work out between her and Tyler, but she refused to be with a liar and a cheat.

Kaiya abruptly changed her mind and drove away. She had more class than to be seen yelling at a cheating man for all and sundry to see. She would give him a piece of her mind as soon as she saw him.

Distraught, Kaiya drove back to the studio in breakneck speed. Thankfully, her helpers wouldn't show up until later at 3 pm when the first dance lessons would start.

Tears stung her eyes, but she refused to shed them. Tyler would never have her tears again. She hastily sniffed them back even though her heart felt as if an invisible hand was squeezing it.

"How could Tyler do this to us?" she questioned continually as she paced her office.

She struggled to give him the benefit of the doubt, but it was fruitless. How would he explain the lunch date?

No wonder he seemed so distracted lately, almost sneaky. Twice he had left her presence to answer a phone call. Was he tired of her already? Had she given in too quickly? But how did one play hide and seek with the man you loved? It didn't make sense.

Unable to hold in her emotions and desiring someone to talk to, she reached for her phone and dialed her sister's number. Unfortunately, it went to voice mail. Then she dialed Jalissa's number. Her best friend didn't answer the call either.

"What's going on? Where's everyone, and why are they not picking up their calls?"

Frustrated, Kaiya gave into the tears that were threatening to burst her tear ducts. She wept at losing the man she loved and the future that she would have had with him. Her day was ruined, and there was nothing she could do about it.

When Tyler dropped off Lili at 5 pm, her second and final dance lesson from the intermediate class, she wanted to throttle him for lying to her.

He had the audacity to move forward to plant a kiss on her lips. Moving away from his intention swiftly, she focused her attention on her daughter. She caught the surprise on his face from the corner of her eye.

Served him right!

The only reason she was silent was because she didn't feel like making a scene in front of her students and, more importantly, their daughter. She had thought long and hard after she contained her tears. She figured she would just try to get some type of custody arrangement, and although it would be hard, she would end things with Tyler.

* * *

"Dammit, what's going on?"

Tyler raked his fingers through his hair as he observed Kaiya's face. When he arrived at the dance school a few hours ago, he had noticed the coldness in her. He had thought she was just having a bad day. But now, hours later, he noticed her bad day was as a result of him.

The woman he loved was relating well with the kids and her employees, but she was treating him as if he had the plague.

Her smiles as she stiltedly talked to him didn't quite reach her eyes. Her words were short and curt. She was putting on an act, and he wondered for the umpteenth time what put her in that mood. He had a huge surprise planned for her, and he didn't want anything to go wrong.

"Is something wrong, Kai?" he asked for the third time, almost at the end of his tether since he didn't know what else to do.

Turning cold eyes on him, she replied, "Stop asking me that question, Tyler. Are you making me out to be a liar? I've told you repeatedly that I'm fine."

"Look, I'm not calling you a liar. You're acting weird, and I'd like to know what's going on."

When she didn't say anything but looked at him as if he wasn't there, he threw up his hands in exasperation.

"Fine. If you say so." He ran his fingers through his hair and said, "Can we at least go for dinner now?"

Watching her shake her head nearly broke his heart. What in the world was going on?

"I'm sorry; I'm not in the mood to going out. I'm exhausted. I just want to go home and sleep."

Tyler was so disappointed; he didn't know what to say. All he wanted to do was fall on his knees and beg her not to do this to him, and whatever he might have done to upset her, he was really sorry. He didn't understand why she was acting this way, and it scared him that she might want out of their relationship.

Or did she find out about the secret party and was only acting out to make things difficult for him? Looking at her impassive face, he didn't think that was the case. If she knew, she ought to be happy, not acting as if she would like to take a stick to him.

"Aww, Mom, please come with us," Lili stepped in and pleaded with her mother.

Tyler could kiss his daughter for her interference, and he did. Lili giggled while Kaiya rolled her eyes.

"Mom, please!" Lili's lips quivered.

"Oh, alright," she finally acquiesced, lifting his heart. "For your sake, sweetie."

He took the insult well. In fact, he would take any insult from her, as long as she accompanied them.

The drive to the hotel was tense and silent. Lili's chatter all the way was the only thing that kept the tension that was rising between the two adults from escalating. Tyler was at his tether's end. If Kaiya was acting as if death warmed over her like this, then the surprise engagement was bound to be a flop. His heart wrenched at the thought that she was most likely to refuse his proposal.

"Mom, are you okay?" Lili finally asked after she had tried to coerce her mom into talking to no avail.

Tyler almost kissed his daughter again as he waited for Kaiya to answer.

Kaiya turned on her seat to bestow her daughter with a warm smile—a smile he hadn't received all day.

"I'm fine, sweetie. I just had a long day."

Tyler hoped the long day would end beautifully for her. All day he had thought that everything would be perfect. He hadn't thought that the star of the day would lose all her twinkle.

His lips moved in silent prayer that everything would turn out as he hoped.

169

* * *

Keep it together, Kaiya. Don't show him how much he hurt you with his deceit.

Kaiya said those words repeatedly in her mind as Tyler drove the car to the restaurant where they were going to have dinner. Her heart yearned for her to hold him and beg him not to leave her for Erin, but her head told her to get a hold on herself. She couldn't beg for his love. It wouldn't work if he was with her out of pity or for Lili's sake.

Kaiya's jaw dropped when Tyler pulled up at the parking lot of the same hotel she saw him and Erin coming out of.

The gall and hide of him!

Unable to stop herself, she said in between clenched teeth, "Can I see you outside for a minute, Tyler?" Then she turned to her daughter with a smile that she hoped the little girl wouldn't see as forced. "Sweetie, could you please wait here while I talk to your dad for a minute?"

Shrugging, Lili reached for the radio's knob to turn it up and sing along with Jasmine's and Aladdin's song.

"Okay, Mommy."

Without looking in Tyler's direction, she removed her seatbelt, pushed open the car door, and stepped away from the vehicle. Tyler did the same and came around the car to look at her inquisitively.

"What's up, Kai?"

"What's up is you playing a two-timing game with me!"

His forehead creased in a frown. "What are you talking about?"

Folding her arms across her chest and giving him a look filled with disdain, she said, "I saw you and Erin coming out of this hotel looking all cozy, laughing and smiling at each other."

She had expected him to look guilty, not relieved. Her brows shot up when she heard him exhale loudly.

"So, that's what has you in a terrible mood." He laughed shortly and drew closer. She took a step back and gave him a contemptuous stare.

He raised his hands in a gesture of pleading. "Please, Kai. You just have to trust me."

"Trust you?" She laughed without mirth. "I did, but you threw it back in my face."

"There's nothing going on between Erin and I. I'll explain everything if you'll just come with me."

"Why should I do that?"

"Kai, please. For the sake of the love we share and for our daughter, just come with me."

Kaiya allowed that she couldn't continue standing out there arguing with him, so she shrugged without relaxing her features. She decided to go with faith and trust him.

Tyler helped his daughter from the vehicle and walked with them to the hotel's dining room. Kaiya was stunned because the place was dark except for a spotlight.

What's going on?

Tyler walked her and Lili to the spotlight. He got down on one knee and brought down a ring from his pocket and raised it.

"Oh, my God." Her breath came in fast. She and her daughter shared dazzling smiles.

"Kaiya, finding you again has been one of the highlights of my life. You gave me a beautiful daughter, and you brought unrestrained happiness back into my life. I love you, and I want to spend the rest of my life with you. Kai, will you marry me?"

"Oh, my God!" Her hands went to her mouth. This was her dream come true. She didn't care that it didn't happen the way she would have liked —with them raising their daughter from birth and maybe on baby number three or four by now. She was happy; she loved their daughter and their life now.

"Yes. Yes. I'll marry you, Tyler!" There was no point taking a moment to think about it. This was what she wanted. What she always wanted.

He rose to his feet, slipped the ring into her finger, and kissed her passionately. She hugged him and her daughter when he pulled away.

Suddenly the light came on, and she was stunned to see Tyler's mom, her sister, Finn and their children as well as Jalissa, Justin and his twin Violet as well as her coworkers standing in a corner. Erin was also present in giving applause.

Tyler whispered to her that Erin had been helping him plan this engagement party and wedding.

"Wedding?"

Before he could reply, Jalissa and Kalilah interrupted them and whisked her and Lili away from Tyler.

"Congratulations!" They said in unison.

Smiling brightly and turning around to look at her fiancé who blew her a kiss, Kaiya asked, "Where are we going?"

"To get you and your daughter dressed for your wedding."

They led her into the elevator and into an exquisite room where they showed her a glamorous fishtail wedding dress adorned with pearls.

Jalissa came to take a closer look at Kaiya's engagement ring as Kalilah helped do Kaiya's hair.

"Wow!" Jalissa exclaimed as she stared at the diamond ring. "If this is the engagement ring, I can't wait to see the wedding band."

Kaiya giggled, looking at the large stone that graced her finger. Love for Tyler poured out of her. To think she had spent almost all day in misery thinking their relationship was over while he was trying to make today perfect for her. Her happiness over the turn of events radiated through her.

Kaiya and Lili got dressed up quickly. Both dresses were made from white satin. Kaiya's dress was long and tight-fitting with a long-sleeved lace bodice, Lili's dress was a knee-length princess dress with a scooped neck. After ensuring that they both looked good, the women returned to the lobby so that Kaiya could get married to the love of her life, the father of her baby, and the man of her dreams in the presence of her family.

Kaiya was finally joined to Tyler in holy matrimony in the exquisite hotel. During the celebration, Kaiya noticed Jalissa and Justin sneaking away. She shook her head with a grin on her face. She was happy to see that Jalissa and Justin were still sneaking around, but she also knew her best friend. Justin's time in Jalissa's bed was almost up. She hoped that it wouldn't cause a rift in the family.

"I'm so sorry for doubting your love and faithfulness to me," she told her husband as they had their first dance as a couple.

He shrugged, smiling. "Considering all our past misunderstandings, I understand, but I need you to trust that I will never hurt you. You and our daughter mean the world to me. This is our second chance, and I don't intend on taking it for granted."

"I trust you, Ty, and I love you," she declared with pent-up emotion. "Thanks for making me the happiest woman in the world."

"Thank you, too, for accepting me. I love you."

Epilogue

Three Months Later...

Chuckling, Tyler watched his wife as she closed her eyes tautly.
"Are you going to read it or not?" he asked when she still didn't open her eyes after a few minutes.

"It isn't time yet," she replied, biting the insides of her cheek.

He rolled his eyes. "Babe, it's over five minutes now."

"Really? I thought it was just a minute."

Laughing, he reached for the test strip she was holding tautly in her hand. "Do you want me to read it?"

Her tongue darted across her lips. "Yes, please."

He tried to take it from her, but she still held on firmly to it. "Babe, please let go."

Exhaling loudly, she softened her grip, and he took the test trip from her. Letting out a breath he didn't know he had been holding, he looked at it, and elation went through him.

"It's positive!"

"What!" Her eyes opened and enlarged.

They were on a Disney cruise honeymooning with their daughter. Kaiya had decided to take a test since she didn't feel well. He had not been surprised that she had even come with the test strips. They've been spending most of their free time in bed with no protection. Kaiya had moved into his house and his mom had moved into Kaiya's condo to give them privacy.

"You're pregnant!"

"Are you sure?" she questioned as she took the test strip from him. Her eyes widened. "I am! We're going to have a baby!"

He drew her into his arms and kissed her until they were both breathless. Her eyes glazed and took on a faraway look. He knew she was remembering when she discovered she was pregnant with Lili. Kaiya had begun talking to her parents again recently since he kept his end of the deal. He no longer felt guilty. Everything that happened brought them to this new chapter. He didn't want to dwell on things he couldn't change... Lili had asked to meet her grandparents and they had allowed it.

Richard who never directly apologized to Kaiya for taking her child away from her, did apologize to his granddaughter when she asked him why he didn't want her in his life. It was an emotional day to see Richard's reaction to the young girl. As for her mom, she had apologized profusely to her daughter and expressed how much she missed spending time with her. Kaiya confided in Tyler that her feelings about what her dad did and then her mom's omission still made her feel uneasy, although she decided to finally move on from it. She generally kept her distance from them even though she knew how much it hurt her mom.

Tyler had a feeling that this was his wife's payback, but she denied that it was. His wife confessed that she couldn't bring herself to be close to her mother again. Kaiya and Tyler allowed her parents access to Lili, as long as the little girl was with her aunt Kalilah and her cousins. They didn't want their daughter to harbor any hatred in her young heart towards her grandparents.

He cradled her face and placed a kiss on her forehead. "Don't think about it, babe. This time around, we're going to create pleasant memories to replace the previous one."

She nodded with tears in her eyes. "I can't wait to tell Lili. Now she'll stop with the insinuations of us giving her a baby brother."

Tyler laughed with gusto. "She's going to be overjoyed." He cuddled her into his embrace. "I love you, babe. Forever and always. I can't wait to meet the addition to our family."

Smiling, she replied, "Me neither."

His hand went to her stomach where his child nestled. "I think it's going to be a boy."

Kaiya threw back her head with joyous laughter. "Oh, really?"

He laughed again and locked lips with hers. Just then, her phone started ringing. She wrenched her lips from his, and he grumbled.

"Leave it," he demanded as his hand reached for her breasts.

"It might be important. I'll tell the person to call back later."

"Then you might as well allow it go to voicemail." He kneaded her breasts, and thrills went up his body.

"Ty!"

"Oh, alright! I'll be right here waiting for you." He brushed past her to enter their large cabin bedroom.

His wife laughed as she followed him in and shut the bathroom door. She reached for her phone on the dresser and frowned.

"What?" he questioned as he laid on the bed, a tender smile on his face.

"It's my sister." She shrugged and answered it.

He jolted from the bed when her eyes enlarged, and then tears filled them. By the time she lowered the phone, tears were rolling down her face.

"It's Ja...Lissa," her sobs were louder now. "She's bee...been hurt. They don't think she'll make it."

Author's Notes

Thank you for reading **Love Interrupted**. This book has taken me almost a year to complete, and I hope you enjoyed seeing Kaiya, Tyler, and Lili get their happily ever after. The love they have for each other really does transcend every obstacle that was placed in their path. Look out for Jalissa and Justin's story in the summer of 2020.

There are so many people that I have to thank.

My fantastic editor - Tanisha, who answers all my weird questions at weird times during the day. Thank you. Your guidance and help on this journey has been insanely helpful, and it is much appreciated.

My amazing beta readers Helena M, Simone C, and Lawander H. You ladies are the best! Thank you for your critical feedback!

Last but certainly not least, my awesome readers. Thank you for the continued support. I appreciate it immensely. Without you, I wouldn't be on this journey.

Thank you again for reading this book. I would really appreciate it if you left me a review on amazon. Reviews help authors and help other readers to find books.

***

If you would like to be kept up to date on new releases and giveaways, please like my Facebook page Niomie Roland or follow me on Instagram @NiomieRoland.

Other Books By The Author

Sold To The Highest Bidder

Desperate to buy the bakery where she slaved over for years, Nazalie decides to auction off the only thing she owns that is worth something: Her virginity.

My Wife's Baby

An unplanned pregnancy leads a young couple down a dark path, which leaves them reeling when they find out the truth behind the origins of the pregnancy.

Anderson Sisters Series

Claiming His Wife (Anderson Sisters Book 1)

A young wife returns home with one thing on her mind. Divorce. Her husband, however, won't make it easy for her to walk away from him that easily.

What Happens In Vegas Series

Jessa & Jaxon

She was in Las Vegas for her best friend's bachelorette party. Everything changed when her eyes met those of a familiar stranger's across the bar. Now she was legally attached to someone who had no intention of letting her go.

Meesha & Connor

When she returned from her Vegas bachelerotte party, she had no idea her wedding would be canceled and someone she met in Vegas would follow her home and become her nightmare.

Jasmine & Antonio

When she bumped into her best friend's stepbrother in Vegas, she had no idea that one night of unbridled passion, would have lasting consequences.

Holiday Romances

Christmas Ever After

When a frightful encounter culminates into Trinity and Michael meeting, he brings forth a proposition. With Christmas on the horizon, will Trinity jump at the opportunity Michael presented her?

Made in the USA
Middletown, DE
24 April 2023

29426025R00106